GUNFIRE LAND

GUNFIRE LAND

JACKSON COLE

WHEELER
CHIVERS

This Large Print edition is published by Wheeler Publishing, Waterville, Maine, USA and by AudioGO Ltd, Bath, England.
Wheeler Publishing, a part of Gale, Cengage Learning.
The text of this Large Print edition is unabridged.
Other aspects of the book may vary from the original edition.
Set in 16 pt. Plantin.

LIBRARY OF CONGRESS CATALOGING-IN-PUBLICATION DATA
Cole, Jackson.
Gunfire land / by Jackson Cole. — Large print ed.
p. cm. — (Wheeler Publishing large print western)
ISBN-13: 978-1-4104-3982-6 (pbk.)
ISBN-10: 1-4104-3982-8 (pbk.)
1. Large type books. I. Title.
PS3505.O2685G86 2011
813'.52—dc22   2011017528

BRITISH LIBRARY CATALOGUING-IN-PUBLICATION DATA AVAILABLE

Published in 2011 in the U.S. by arrangement with Golden West Literary Agency.
Published in 2012 in the U.K. by arrangement with Golden West Literary Agency.

U.K. Hardcover: 978 1 445 83842 7 (Chivers Large Print)
U.K. Softcover: 978 1 445 83843 4 (Camden Large Print)

Printed in the United States of America
1 2 3 4 5 6 7 15 14 13 12 11

GUNFIRE LAND

CHAPTER I:
WELL OF DEATH

The wind across the Trans-Pecos brought no relief, only accentuating the blistering, dry heat. Prickly pear, mesquite, Spanish bayonet, the ocotillo with its graceful wand-flowers, were coated with gray dust, and the tough clump grasses rustled thirstily in the breeze.

Water was scarce and worth anything in this part of Texas. Miles east of the spot, the black-watered Pecos River ran through its deep, tortuous canyon, denying the parched roots its vital moisture as it held its tributaries far below the surface in small, inaccessible ravines. Ranchers had to pump up their water. The scattered water-holes were few and far between. Here and there wells had been dug, although the underground flow was deep down and in many places could not be tapped.

But Bob Allison was used to this sered universe. In fact, he liked it, just as he enjoyed his work as a cowhand, and swift, hard riding. He had been born and bred in Southwest Texas, across the Pecos, and love of the land was in his blood, pioneer blood that flowed in his warm young veins.

They were digging a new well, some miles from "Big Ed" Lee's Square L ranchhouse, a well they hoped would serve the cattle in this section so that the creatures would not run off all their fat by going miles for a drink.

Allison was helping Jack Lee, son of the Square L, and Allison's best friend. Half a dozen Mexicans were doing the shovel work, but Allison and Lee now and then would grow impatient and jump in and make the clay fly themselves.

Around the depression where they labored were crested hills, covered with scrub trees and chaparral, and with jagged red rocks showing through.

Huge and broad-shouldered, Allison was a Texas man whose light hair grew crisp under his curved wide Stetson, and whose brown eyes which looked straight at a man were quick to mirth. He had a good nose and a strong jaw — a handsome young fellow in his blue shirt and leather riding pants.

Jack Lee was slimmer, darker of hair and skin. When he was smiling, as he usually

8

was, his white teeth gleamed. The two young fellows were always joking, laughing together, for theirs was a deep friendship. It had been more firmly cemented when Allison had fallen in love with Jack's young sister, Doris. In fact, he had taken the job at the Square L after he had met Doris at a dance in Pecosville, the town serving the range.

"Doggone these fellows, Bob!" Lee exclaimed. "All they want to do is take siestas. No wonder we haven't got far."

A pile of gravel and clay stood nearby, hoisted from the hole by a bucket windlass. They had made about thirty feet, but as yet there was no sign of moisture. However, they had hopes of striking water at fifty or sixty feet. Now there was nothing except the plank shoring that stuck up around the sides of the hole. Shovels and picks and gear lay about. And in some shade patches near at hand were the horses of the workers.

"Here comes George Canty, Jack," Allison said, looking beyond the well.

Lee turned, and both young men watched as several riders came down the south slope into the depression and cantered over to them.

"Howdy, gents," the man in the lead greeted. Three heavy-muscled, flat-skulled fellows were with him.

"Afternoon, Canty," Lee replied carelessly.

George Canty was a raw-boned man with a tremendous torso. The muscles corded out from under his shirt sleeves and from his crooked back — overdeveloped muscles because of his work, for he was a professional well-digger. His legs, gripping the black mustang he rode, were thin for such a heavy body, and scanty, coarse red hair showed on his leonine head when he pushed back his black hat.

And he had a habit of cocking his head to one side, on his thick neck, so that he appeared to be looking slantwise at Allison and Jack Lee. His features were freckled, deep-burned by the Texas sun; reddish beard stubble stuck out on his flat cheeks. His mouth was wide, the lips a thin, straight line, and his eyes had a greenish tinge.

Canty was known to be something of a queer character, selfconscious, and with a picturesquely profane vocabulary.

"What in thunder you boys doin'?" Canty demanded from the side of his wide mouth. "Headin' for China?" He winked, showing yellow buck teeth as he grinned.

"We're after water," Allison said, without grinning.

Jack Lee only laughed up at the strange

Canty. Canty blinked, his lips tightening. He had a glorified opinion of himself, but sometimes thoughtless cowboys jibed or laughed at him and he never liked it. They called him "Crab," too, because he walked with a sideward shuffle. Digging water wells since he was a youth had affected his physical appearance.

With a characteristic curse, Canty dismounted. From his saddle-bag he took a forked stick.

"You younkers got no sense," he growled, gripping the forks of the peeled stick.

Allison and Lee watched interestedly, as did their Mexicans. Canty muttering to himself, eyes closed, walked about with the stick firmly clasped in his hairy, calloused hands. The muscles of his forearms bulged with his grip, and the bottom branch of the Y stick was up. Some of the Mexicans looked nervous, for, though they knew of it, what Canty was doing smacked of magic to them.

Back and forth and across the depression walked Canty, lips moving, the forked stick not changing its position in his hands, held before him. After several minutes Canty stopped, opened his eyes, and dropped the stick from its upright position.

"You boys are fools," he said contemptuously. "Ain't no water in this hole."

"Why?" asked Lee, obviously amused. "Just 'cause yore stick didn't drop?"

Canty grew tremendously excited. "Sneerin' at the stick, won't find water, Lee. It's the best witch-hazel wood and it's never failed! Goes down like steel to a magnet if there's any water underneath — that is, within diggin' distance. Yore old man's tryin' to save a few dollars by not hirin' me to dig his wells, but he'll lose more in time and money when yuh boys hit it dry. No young whipper-snappers can beat me! I savvy my business."

"Then go ahead and mind it, Canty," Jack Lee advised shortly. "Yuh give us a raw deal on that last job yuh done for us — cheated Dad — so it's yore last. C'mon fellers, keep diggin'."

A dark flush showed beneath Canty's bronzed, freckled skin, and his eyes narrowed. His feelings were easily hurt. With a profane snarl he leaped on his horse and, followed by his men, swiftly rode off.

"He's sore 'cause he didn't get this job," remarked Jack. "Ain't he a funny-lookin' hombre, Bob? He does move like a big crab, like they say."

They went on working for another hour, when Allison threw down his shovel.

12

"What say we lay off for dinner, Jack? I'm dry, and I'm starved. Let's take our chow and eat it in the shade of them live-oaks on the hill."

"All right."

Lee called a halt which the Mexicans instantly appreciated, dropping their tools. They congregated together, chattering, smoking, pulling bottles of *tequila* from under shading rocks.

Lee and Allison got their food from their saddle-bags, and their canteens, and walked to the slope. In the deep shade of the oaks on the ridge the breeze felt a bit cooler. The grandiose sweep of the land, with mountains in the distance, and red buttes protruding from the cactus-studded flats, the brassy sky, made an impressive picture, too.

"I'd like to make El Paso for the Harvest Festival, Bob," Jack Lee remarked. "There's a rodeo and the senoritas there are the prettiest in the county. If Dad'll let me, I'm goin'. How about comin' along?"

"Well, I'd like to, Jack," Allison confessed. "It would be good fun. But do yuh think yore dad means to go? I mean —"

Young Lee burst into laughter, pounding his friend between the shoulder-blades.

"Oh, I know you, yuh old rascal. I know

yuh wouldn't leave here unless Doris went, too!"

Allison grinned sheepishly, because he knew that was true. He had no desire to go away from the Square L, and leave Doris there.

As they opened the lunches Doris had fixed for them early that morning when they had left the ranch Jack said ruefully: "Say, yores looks better'n mine. Sis ain't fair."

"Yes, she is —" began Allison, then stopped and laughed.

Hard work had given them good appetites, and they quickly consumed all the food in sight. Then they rolled cigarettes.

"Life ain't so bad, is it?" Jack Lee said musingly, blowing out a cloud of bluish-gray smoke.

His dark eyes sought the distances, and his nostrils widened to the aromatic, dryly keen air. Good health and youth brought natural joy and Jack Lee was a fine young man, ready and willing to work hard at any job. He had the Texan's quick temper but Allison knew there was not a mean bone in his young wiry body.

"It's mighty good," Allison answered gravely.

"Do you —" began Lee.

He stopped, checked short with what

14

sounded like a gasp. For a second, Allison didn't realize what had happened. Then, staring at Jack, he saw that his friend's mouth and eyes were wide and that he was sinking to the warm earth.

"Hey, Jack — what's wrong?" shouted Allison.

His heart gave a terrible flip of anxiety. But he didn't comprehend what actually had happened until he saw the blood spurting from Lee's side, under the heart.

Bob Allison, frantic with alarm now, leaped to his feet. Just as he moved, however, something hit him. It was as though a giant hand had suddenly seized his shoulder and spun him around. The shock took away his breath, and a paralyzing pain streaked through him. He landed on the hard dirt, trying to cry out, but unable to.

It was an instant before he realized he, too, had been shot, for he had heard no sounds. His eyes happened to fix on the south, on a red-rock butte a couple of hundred yards away. The sunlight glinted on metal there and in the nightmare confusion of the moment, Allison had the impression of a reddish-haired, twisted head.

Another bullet from the rifle whirled close over him as he lay there. Then he got hold of young Lee's leg and pulled as he rolled

15

off the crest of the hill, seeking to get the top between them and the gunman behind the butte.

His whole left side felt dead, paralyzed, after the first telegraphed pain.

He tried to shout, to call the Mexicans. He heard a sound then as a heavy bullet whined up, striking a rock. He heard the strange *whoop-whoo-op* of the ricochet.

Allison fought for consciousness. Only vaguely he realized that Jack was gone, must have died when the first shot hit him. Rolling, crawling, Allison made a few yards, and the butte was no longer visible. Down below him was the depression with the new well, and now the Mexicans had heard the shooting and were starting to run toward him.

He pushed up to his feet with his uninjured right hand, staggered down the slope a few yards to meet them, trying to call out. The world danced crazily before his eyes, and he fell face down. He slid a short distance and crumpled up.

CHAPTER II:
FORCED ALIBI

When Bob Allison came to, he was lying on his back on the front of the great Spanish veranda which ran around three sides of the Square L house, built in *hacienda* style of white-washed adobe bricks. Commodious and cool, the thick-walled, airy home defied even the blistering sun of the Trans-Pecos.

The first thing he heard was a girl's broken-hearted sobbing. He forced open his tortured eyes to see Doris Lee, the girl he loved, crouched near him, crying. She was beside her dead brother. Evidently the Mexicans had brought Jack's body when they had carried the unconscious Allison to the ranchhouse.

A big man whose pepper-and-salt locks showed beneath a fawn Stetson stood by the railing, his legs spread and booted feet planted, staring down at his dead son, and fighting for control. Big Ed Lee, owner of the Square L and father of Jack and Doris,

17

was stricken. For once the big Colts at his waist were of no use to him. For he had received the worst blow that can befall a man.

His close-clipped dark mustache was beginning to turn gray, his nose and mouth were strong, and his black eyes were deep-set and handsome. But he was a forlorn man now, for Lee's love for his family was deep and abiding, and to lose one of his loved ones was bitter. He adored his children, and for them he had torn the Square L from a harsh wilderness.

"Doris — Doris!" Allison whispered.

He realized that his wound had been bandaged, and that his lips were wet. Even their grief had not made them forget to give him a drink.

The girl turned to him, a small but exquisitely formed girl in the first wonderful flush of her twentieth year. Her hair was raven-black, catching the light with a sheen. The long lashes over her lovely violet eyes were wet with tears now, and her red lips quivered.

"Bob!" she choked. "You're not going to. . . . Oh, you *must* get well!"

"I'm goin' to," he assured. "I don't think I was hit too bad. Jack —"

"Gone!" she quavered, and he nodded soberly.

"Yeah, I know."

When he heard Allison's voice, Big Ed Lee seemed to start from a trance. He stepped to Allison's side, holding himself tense, with an iron command. His fingers dug into the palms of his large hands. His handsome head, crowned by the fawn-hued hat, was proudly held. He was a cattle king, accustomed to giving orders and having them implicitly obeyed, accustomed to having his own way. Allison admired Lee and knew no finer man ever rode the range than the boss, but Lee was a broken man now, for the moment.

"Who done it, Bob?" demanded Lee, in a tight, husky voice. "The Mexes say they don't savvy, didn't see anybody."

"I'd swear it was George Canty," Allison said hoarsely. "He come to our camp and he was sore 'cause yuh hadn't give him the well-diggin' job. An hour or so after he left, Jack and I went to the crest to eat lunch. A bullet killed Jack — and I *know* I glimpsed Canty, firin' from behind a butte! Then he winged me."

"Canty! Curse him! He'll pay for this if I have to turn the whole state of Texas upside down!" Big Ed Lee swore whole-heartedly.

A wagon came chattering into the yard, beyond which were the corrals, the bunkhouse, and stables, with gear and appendages around, all the needed apparatus for running such a spread. Dust billowed up as the cowboy driver jerked the buckboard to a stop.

A woman threw herself from the seat and hurried to the porch, a woman of middle age, whose eyes were wide with horror, misery. "My boy — Jack!" she gasped.

Big Ed Lee took his wife in his arms, trying to comfort her. . . .

As soon as the two young ranchmen had fallen, George Canty rode hard, picking up his men as he spurred his rangy black mustang south away from the spot where he had shot Jack Lee and Bob Allison.

"You boys keep yore traps shut, savvy!" he growled to the three who had been with him when he had killed.

Those three were his most faithful retainers. They were not strong on brains, but they swore by Canty, who paid them. Moreover, Canty knew interesting things about each. The one with one eye who wore a patch over his other, had killed a man in an El Paso saloon brawl. The thin one with the crooked nose was wanted for highway robbery in three separate Texas counties. The fat, short fellow was a notorious rustler, a fugitive from the Border.

Canty led the way, his twisted lips working as he talked to himself:

"Curse it all, that Allison shifted just as I shot — don't believe I finished him. Did he see me when I rose up to fire ag'in? Yes, he must have! Why didn't I go back and clean out them Mexes? No, one would've shore got away — they're good riders."

He was greatly agitated, not because of the murders he had done but at the possible consequences to himself. He calmed himself by the assurance that he had had to kill the two young men.

"Laughed at me, they did." His teeth gritted, his eyes blinked. "Should I run for it? No, I'll be blasted if I do! I won't quit. I'll cover up, one way or another!"

He was already planning how he would do that. He had been alone when he had committed the murders for he left his men a couple of miles away, to sneak back and drygulch Lee and Allison. Had he killed Allison, there would be no witness or evidence against him. But if Allison lived, and talked, Canty knew he must be prepared for arrest.

He swung on, with his men, and in the late afternoon, they pulled up at a small ranch belonging to a man Canty knew —

Duke Varron. It was a shabby rundown place, of board and brick and odds-and-ends, unpainted. Some men in leather range clothing lounged in the shade, and Canty nodded shortly to them.

"Is Duke home?" he asked them.

"Yeah, he's inside."

Canty dismounted from his lathered horse and shuffled to the porch, went up the steps. His men turned off toward the water trough at the rear.

"Why, howdy, Canty!" called a man from the shadowed interior. His voice sounded apprehensive and he rose quickly, facing the well-digger. "Have a seat, will yuh?"

Canty pulled up a chair, and Duke Varron resumed his seat. Canty stared straight into Varrun's shifty black eyes.

Varron, in well-fitting shirt and corduroys, was handsome in an oily way. His body was supple and slim, and sleek sideburns curved low over his olive-skinned cheeks. He had a dandy's tiny mustache over a weak mouth.

Duke Varron's reputation, while not exactly tarnished in the district, could have been better. It was whispered that at one time he had been handy with the long rope and running-iron, but he had never been caught in the act. He had fifteen or twenty riders working for him, and more at times.

His brand was a Lazy C, which he had bought, and while he had steers on the range he never seemed to work too hard at ranching.

"What's up?" he asked Canty, licking his lip.

"I need yore help, Varron. I just shot Jack Lee and Bob Allison."

Varron jumped violently.

"Killed 'em?"

"I killed Lee. I ain't shore of Allison. And that's why I'm here. Yuh got a couple of hombres we can trust to the limit?"

Duke Varron dropped his eyes, feigning to be examining his long nails. "Why, I reckon so, Canty. But — murder ain't so nice!"

A flush mantled the well-digger's dark hide. He had a commanding nature, and as Varron felt Canty's rage mounting, Duke began to crawfish.

"You ain't hardly in a position to refuse me help, Duke," Canty growled.

"Oh, I ain't refusin', Canty," Duke said hastily. "Anything yuh say."

Canty seized Varron's bony wrist in a steel grip.

"Now listen, close, Duke. I need an iron-clad alibi, savvy? It ain't just a question of coverin' what I done today. I'll tell yuh why I shot Lee and Allison — it was a danged *good* reason! — and I'm goin' to let yuh in on the biggest propersition yuh ever hoped to hear. We're goin' on, and there'll be more jobs to do on the order of this one. Are yuh game?"

Duke Varron's eyes shone. He licked his lips greedily, for any mention of prospective wealth always excited him. "All right," he said. "I'm with yuh to the hilt, Canty."

"Good. I'm goin' in and surrender to Sheriff Miles tonight. Meanwhile, we'll work it all out so it's airtight."

Death and destruction hung over the range, as Canty gave his orders. . . .

That was the situation, months later, when reports of actual death and terror began to seep into Texas Rangers Headquarters in the state's capital.

CHAPTER III:
RANGE WAR

"Range war!" growled Captain Bill McDowell, reading the reports that had just come in, at his desk in the Austin Headquarters of the Texas Rangers. "There ain' nothin' worse! And this is a specially nasty one!"

Fifty years of law work as a Texas Ranger had endowed Captain Bill with the faculty of judging such affairs, even from hundreds of miles away. Also he knew that in the business of enforcing the law nothing called for such skill and courage as did the settling of a range feud.

They had a way of starting, perhaps from a hasty word or an angry blow, in one spot. Then, like a match flame whipped up by a strong wind, they would sweep out terrifyingly, spreading until whole counties were involved and death struck wholesale.

It took a man with icy nerve, and with a swift, keen mind to check such a conflagration of human emotions, to ferret out the truth. But Cap McDowell knew such a man.

He banged the bell on his desk and his orderly jumped to the doorway, looking like a scared rabbit. When Cap'n Bill was in a temper, the fur was likely to fly.

"Tell Ranger Hatfield to step in here, cuss it!"

McDowell jumped up, too impulsively. He grimaced as his lame back caught him with paralyzing agony. His spirit was as fierce and ready as ever but his physical shell which no longer permitted him to ride the danger trails even refused to allow him to express his excitement — bodily.

A soft tread sounded and McDowell turned to face the young man who entered the office. The captain's seamed face relaxed as his keen blue eyes rested on the Ranger he had picked for this job across the Pecos. Though he himself stood six feet in his stocking feet, McDowell had to glance up to catch the gaze of the tall officer who answered his call.

"Hatfield!" exclaimed Cap'n Bill. "Yuh're just back from a devilish hard job, I know, but now I got a tougher one. But Jones is down on the Gulf Coast, Arrington's busy as a one-armed paperhanger in the Panhandle. Young Miller's in, but he ain't much experienced yet. So —"

"What is it, Cap'n," asked Hatfield quietly. His voice was drawling, gentle. "You savvy I'd rather ride than sit any time."

"Well sit a minute, anyways, and we'll go over it. Young Hades has popped loose in Reeves, across the Pecos."

Jim Hatfield, listening, was an imposing figure of a man. He was breath-taking in size, with wide shoulders tapering to the lean waist of the ace fighting man. A studded belt supported walnut-stocked Colt .45s, in oiled, supple black holsters. He wore spurred halfboots, leather chaps over corduroys, and a red shirt. A wide Stetson was perched on the raven-black hair of his rugged head.

Stern as his features were, they were softened by a fine wide mouth that showed his innate good humor. And in that long body was the rippling power of a panther, and his straight-forward gaze showed that his heart beat with a steady courage that never knew the quavering check of fear.

McDowell knew that this man had nerves of steel and the speed of leger-demain in a fight. But what made him so valuable, and rare, was that he was the possessor of the most logical mind McDowell had ever encountered, a brain that was sure and keen, never heated in a rage, but always cool and able to function at its best.

Shaded by long, dark lashes, Hatfield's gray-green eyes seemed lazy, now. But they could cloud up and be as icy-seeming as an Arctic sea darkened by a storm. Then whoever was responsible for that had best turn, and run. For from the Kansas line to the Rio Grande, from El Paso to the Gulf, Jim Hatfield was known as the finest Texas Ranger in the Lone Star State.

Ever since Hatfield had joined Cap'n McDowell's forces and the fighting chief had been unable to go out on such missions himself, McDowell had dispatched Hatfield on his most dangerous law work. He had been well aware that the honor of the Texas Rangers could never be placed in better hands.

Hatfield absorbed the information Mc-Dowell gave him silently, as his chief explained in rapid, terse sentences:

"Nearest town's Pecosville, west of the main stream, Jim," McDowell said. "Cow country as yuh savvy. Got a report from Sheriff Frank Miles, good enough lawman I've dealt with afore. War's flared between two factions. One's Big Ed Lee of the Square L and his pards. Other side's headed by an hombre named George Canty, who digs water-wells. His headquarters is in town, but fightin' along with him is one Duke Varron, a rancher.

"Lee accuses Canty of drygulchin' his son. There was a trial, but Canty was acquitted. But accordin' to Sheriff Miles, Lee won't let it rest. Guns are poppin' and it's shapin' up to one thunderation of a time. I got wires from both Canty and Lee, each complainin' of the other. Lee claims the law was cheated, and Canty that Lee's persecutin' him. Get over there and find the answer. Check it 'fore it's too big to handle and folks die wholesale."

"Yes, sir, Cap'n." Hatfield nodded gently. He rose, towering in the office.

"Wait a jiffy." Cap McDowell held up a hand. "Feller named Jake Barry over there, an old trail-driver and pard of mine, yuh can trust to the hilt. Barry founded Pecosville and owns most of it. He's mayor of the place. Good luck, and *adios*."

McDowell watched as the tall Ranger slipped from the room and went out into the bright sunlight. In the shade, at a hitchrack, stood a magnificent golden gelding, Hatfield's own mount and friend of the trails. The man spoke to the animal caressingly, and Goldy shook his handsome mane, a shade lighter in hue than his beautiful, sleek hide. Hatfield kept him elegantly groomed, and tended his horse before himself.

Saddled up, and with a short-barreled carbine stuck in the boot, with saddlebags filled with iron rations, spare belts filled with cartridges depending from the horn, Jim Hatfield mounted, and started west for the dangerous, black-watered Pecos.

"I hope," thought McDowell, watching the rider disappear, "I don't live to see the day when they don't come back!"

The rushing, black waters of the Pecos and its perilous canyon lay behind the golden sorrel and his great rider, Jim Hatfield. They were moving on the final lap of their journey to Pecosville, where the Ranger meant to consult Mayor Jake Barry and get further details of the war that had flared up.

This country was familiar to Hatfield, the Trans-Pecos. It was semi-arid, the draws choked with mesquite and cactus. Tough grasses flourished, however, and the range could support, with supplementary irrigations, much cattle.

Most of the tributary streams of the vampire Pecos ran in narrow, deep canyons, like the mother river, and were of no use to the roots of the vegetation. Water-holes, and pools were scarce. But the contours were magnificent to the eye, mountains and buttes rising before the horseman on that tremendous plateau.

Rider and mount were not as spick-and-span as they had been when they had left Austin. Gray dust coated them, and the long thorns of the region had caught at their flesh. Goldy had, however, with his tireless stride, made a record run over.

It was late afternoon and the sun was in Hatfield's eyes as he rode. An aromatic, warm wind blew gratefully in his widened nostrils.

Suddenly Goldy rippled his hide, always a warning signal to his rider, and Hatfield narrowed his lids, seeking what the horse sensed that he had not.

"Don't — please!" he heard an agonized voice cry. "I don't —"

The breeze died away, tantalizingly, and Hatfield swung off the beaten trail, carefully watching for the men who must be somewhere before him.

The open trail swung a bend, through two bluffs, but the Ranger put the sorrel to the slope and got up on the higher ground over the way. In a basinlike flat, beyond the ridge that formed the bluffs, he saw four saddled horses standing with their reins on the dry, sandy earth. A hundred yards beyond, under a tall pine tree from which a limb

31

grew handily, twenty feet from the ground, were the men to whom the horses evidently belonged.

Three of the men stood around the fourth, whose neck was decorated by the noose of a long lariat which had been tossed over the pine tree limb. It was held in the hands of a huge fellow in leather chaps and brown shirt, a man who wore a reversed bandanna about a brick-red bull neck and a sand-colored Stetson.

A younger, but almost as large a Texas man, with crisp light hair — he had pushed his hat back off his head — stood at the big man's right, watching. The trio was completed by a thin cowboy.

The victim was a scared-looking fellow with a fat stomach and a round, brown-haired head, and somehow to the watching Ranger neither of his captors appeared to be the type of men who would torture another for nothing. All three of them looked more like sturdy, honest, upstanding Texas men.

As Hatfield came stealthily up behind tall mesquite bushes covering the ridge, the oldest man jerked the rope and for a moment the prisoner danced on air. His hands were not bound and flew to ease the lariat cutting his windpipe.

After that moment, the huge rancher let him down. When he got his breath, the victim screeched:

"Quit it! I — I don't savvy nothin'!"

It was Hatfield's duty to investigate the affair. He could not stand by and see a man lynched. His Ranger badge, the silver star on a silver circle, was snugged in a secret pocket, for it was his habit to look carefully into a case before exposing his real identity. There was nothing to mark him as an officer.

He dismounted, dropped Goldy's reins, and quietly approached, taking a path through the mesquite down the slope.

"Talk, yuh skunk!" roared the elderly cowman.

Like the two cowboys assisting him, he was completely engrossed in the game. A high-powered rifle with special long-range sights lay on the ground near at hand, alongside a cartridge belt containing two smooth-butted Colt pistols.

"I tell yuh I don't savvy anything about it!" wailed the captive desperately, sunk in a heap on the warm earth.

"Yuh savvy they lied themselves blue in the face," stormed the chief of the trio. "I want the truth, Devlin."

Hatfield was now upon them. He could

make out the flushed features of the participants, and see the abject fright in the eyes
of the man called Devlin as the fellow faced
death.

"I'll make the coyote talk!" the huge
rancher snarled. "Pick him up agin, Bob."

The big young man with the light hair and
brown eyes stooped to raise Devlin while
the other man tugged on the rope and
pulled the prisoner up so that his feet were
just barely off the ground. Then one of them
snubbed the other end of the rope around
an exposed root at the base of the tree.

Hatfield liked the appearance of the big
blond young man. He had an open, friendly
countenance, though now he was grave.
Under a coat of heavy tan his cheeks seemed
pallid; as though he had been ill for a long
time and was just recovering. Hatfield liked
the looks of the other men, too — but not
what they were doing.

The men stepped back from the tree leaving Devlin half suspended by the rope, so
that he got a good taste of what it would
mean if he really were left hanging from the
limb.

Hatfield decided the play had to be
checked, while he learned the right and
wrong of it all. This was no doubt part of
the range war he had come to stop, and

these angered ranchers might do something they would later come to regret. Though it might mean antagonizing the three cowmen, Hatfield had to act.

Five yards away, the Ranger straightened up and commanded in a clear, loud voice:

"Hold it, gents!"

CHAPTER IV:
NECKTIE PARTY

In unison the three men swung around. But they stood motionless as they saw Hatfield had them covered with a gun as he advanced directly to the tree. He marched straight to the man Devlin and stood beside the prisoner, still covering the three ranchers with one of his Colts.

"Where in blazes did you come from?" blazed the ranchers' leader with a scowl. "Take my advice — get yore hoss and ride off. This ain't yore affair."

"A necktie party is likely to be anybody's business, sir," drawled Hatfield. "Specially if they ain't shore it's justified."

Hope sprang into Devlin's twisted face. "Don't let 'em string me up, mister!" he cried desperately. "I ain't done nothing, so help me!"

Hatfield drew a large clasp-knife out of his pocket and opened the blade. He was just about to cut the rope when one of the waddies grabbed for his gun. The ranger fired, sending a bullet into the ground at the waddy's feet. The cowboy moved his hand away from his gun butt as though it had bitten him.

"Thanks, mister!" Devlin mumbled gratefully as the knife parted the rope, so that the noose grew slack. "Now just cut my arms free. I was riding to town when they jumped me in the bush."

"Yeah!" sneered the rancher who had bossed the proceedings. "Ridin' to town and takin' pot-shots with a long-range rifle at me on my own range."

Hatfield cut the ropes that bound the prisoner's arms and Devlin pulled the noose off his own neck. He jumped toward the rifle, but Hatfield stopped him.

"Leave that gun alone, pard!" ordered the Ranger. "Get yore hoss and ride off. I'll join yuh later."

Devlin nodded and ran toward his horse. Hatfield had made his play, the best for all concerned, he hoped, and he began backing away from the tree and into the mesquite, still menacing the three men with his gun.

"Nobody'll get hurt if you three hombres stand till we get clear," he called out.

Swiftly he retreated, picking up Goldy. Devlin was riding for the road, low in the saddle of a black mustang. Hatfield followed, calling out to the man he had saved. The other three horses were running off into the brush, for Devlin had stampeded them.

Roars of rage, and revolver fire, came from where Hatfield had left the three ranchers, but the bullets did not come near the Ranger. He glanced back as he high-balled it in Devlin's dust. The big blond cowboy, he saw, had reached the spot where the horses had stood, and was whistling after one. A brown-and-white mustang stopped, turned and trotted obediently back. The blond man swung aboard and rode off full tilt to pick up the other two animals.

Dust showed off to the south now, heading toward the gunfire.

Goldy overtook the black half a mile further on. Devlin winked at him, and grinned.

"Thanks feller," he complimented. "Only yuh should've down them skunks. However, I reckon one would've got yuh 'fore yuh could have finished 'em all. I thought I was a goner."

"Lynchin' yuh, huh?"

"They come close to it."

His nerve returned, Devlin was a different man from the frightened, abject creature

Hatfield had saved. His shifty black eyes gleamed, and not in keeping with the roundness of his head, his nose was sharp, predatory.

"That true, what they said about yuh drygulchin' 'em?" demanded Hatfield.

"Shucks, no," Devlin said, too quickly. "I was peggin' at jack-rabbits, that's all. I was a fool to ride across Square L Range, though. Was on my way to town for a spree and they caught me."

"Square L," repeated Hatfield.

"Yeah, belongs to Big Ed Lee, who thinks he runs this country."

"Who were them fellers with him?"

"Bob Allison and Paul Winters, riders of his'n."

"I shore stepped right into it," thought Hatfield.

The elderly man, then, who had been bossing the near lynching was the Big Ed of whom McDowell had spoken. The blond Allison was the man who had been wounded when Lee's son had been murdered.

The mustang Devlin rode was branded with a Lazy C, and the man saw Hatfield glancing at it inquiringly.

"I work for Duke Varron," Devlin explained. "Him and Lee ain't friendly."

"I gathered that," drawled Hatfield. Devlin kept glancing nervously back.

"What's wrong, Devlin?" Hatfield asked.

"Yuh heard 'em shootin', didn't yuh? Lee never goes out without a bunch of riders to protect him, and his main gang is headin' this way. They wasn't far away just now."

"Huh." Hatfield seemed little interested. "What's the war over — the price of beef?"

"Naw. Lee's loco. He accused a friend of Duke's of shootin' his son. The jury let this hombre, whose handle is Canty, go free, and Lee's riled over it."

Hatfield recalled the rifle belonging to Devlin, a rifle with special sights that he had seen near the spot where Lee and Allison had been stringing up Devlin. He decided that probably Devlin *had* tried to kill them with the long-range weapon.

They came up to a hill crest and searched the ground behind them. Lee, Allison and the waddy who had been with them had come out on the road and were picking up a dozen cowboys who had appeared from the range. The whole party took up the chase of Hatfield and Devlin, who settled down to riding.

But the two had a long start, and kept ahead over rolling country. After an hour, Hatfield saw the town ahead in the little valley, on a brown creek.

"That Pecosville?" he asked Devlin.

"That's her. We're safe now. My boss, Duke, is headin' to town, and if he ain't in yet, we can get other help."

Devlin shook a dirty fist back at the Square L riders who were topping a rise just out of gunshot distance behind.

They galloped down the slope and, hitting the outskirts of the settlement, slowed to a trot.

"I'll buy yuh a drink, big feller," he said. "Yuh've shore earned it." He looked interested. "Goin' far?"

The question was put in a careless tone, but Hatfield knew what it meant. Neither faction would trust a stranger and he had to give a logical explanation of his presence.

"I got an old skinflint of an uncle in town here, Devlin. I ain't seen him since I was a shaver."

"Yeah? What's his handle?"

"Jake Barry."

"Oh, ho!" Devlin's eyes flickered. "The mayor! Yeah, yore uncle's mayor of this shebang and he owns a lot of it. Funny old coot."

"So I heard. But he's sheathed with it, ain't he?" Hatfield hungrily licked his lips. "I wasn't doin' too well where I was and thought I'd might as well come over here as anywhere. It's a long ways from where I happened to be at the time."

"At the time of what?" Devlin laughed and winked at his own joke. "I wish yuh luck with the old boy. What'll I call yuh? I mean, when I interduce yuh."

"Jim — uh — er — Jim Barry'll be fine."

Hatfield sought to give the shifty-eyed Devlin the impression that he had got into trouble and had come to get what he could from his long-lost uncle. Big Ed Lee and Bob Allison would have him marked as a foe, because he had horned in on their game. Devlin, a liar, and by stamp not what the Ranger would call a decent citizen, offered him another tack.

Square L men were doggedly trailing them, and Devlin hurried toward the main section of the town.

"Yeah, there's the boys' hosses over at the Prairie Fire Saloon," he cried.

He pushed up the dusty way, skirting a scrofulous plaza which occupied the center of Pecosville, a typical Southwest range settlement. Main Street was two lines of adobe and rough-board shacks, some with false second-story fronts: stores, and drinking-spots sandwiched between homes. The side roads of rutted dirt, branched off, with buildings along them for a few hundred yards, only to peter out in the chaparral beyond.

The sun was dropping, a huge crimson ball on the horizon, as Hatfield and Devlin approached the Prairie Fire, a large, rambling oasis. The heat of the afternoon hung like a smothering blanket over the town, hemmed in by hills as it was. A small, brown-watered creek was on the west side of the town.

At the hitch-racks, Hatfield noted a score of mustangs with a Lazy C brand on them. Dropping reins over the bar, the Ranger and Devlin ducked under and entered the saloon.

Men were at the bar or sitting at tables scattered about. The smell of wet sawdust and stale whisky permeated the air. The room was shadowed, because lamps were not yet lit. Devlin stepped up to a slim, supple young man wearing a black Stetson and leather.

"Hey, Duke!" he exclaimed. "Here comes the Square L, on our trail! Big Ed Lee grabbed me and tried to lynch me. This hombre with me pulled me out of it and the whole passel run us all the way in."

Swift black eyes searched Devlin's face. Hatfield was certain that the man he had saved gave a quick shake of the head.

Duke Varron's gaze switched to Hatfield. He looked straight into the shaded, gray-green eyes of the Ranger, then as quickly shifted his glance.

"C'mon, boys, the Square L's lookin' for trouble-a-plenty!" shouted Varron, drawing a Colt and jumping out onto the veranda.

His men were efficient-looking fellows, so far as guns were concerned. They were heavily armed, silent, cool, as they trailed him outside. The Square L galloped full-tilt across the plaza, whooping it up and opening fire as they saw their enemies. Colts began to blast, and bullets flew, whistling in the air or drumming into the wooden walls.

Big Ed Lee led his riders on, and kept going. Little damage had been done, and Varron clicked his teeth, licking the little smudge of black mustache on his upper lip.

"That Lee devil and his pards'll get what they're askin' for one of these days," he snapped. "He's got no respect for anything."

The Square L did not return, but rode on north out of town.

"Step in and have a drink, feller," invited Duke, slapping the tall Ranger between the shoulder-blades. "Any pard of Devlin's is a pard of mine, too."

"Don't care if I do," murmured the Ranger, who had fired a couple of shots high over the Square L.

They went back to the bar and began drinking again.

"This feller is Jim Barry, Duke," Devlin informed his boss, jerking a thumb at the Ranger. "He's the mayor's nevvy, but he ain't seen his uncle since he was a pup. He's got plenty nerve. Yuh should've seen the way he faced Lee and Allison down out there."

Hatfield saw Varron start. He was apparently staring at the red depths of the liquor in his glass but he could watch Duke out of the corner of his eye.

"Yuh say yuh're Mayor Barry's nephew?" Varron said, and glanced up at Hatfield.

"Yeah. I ain't shore he'll remember me, though. I better go pay my respects. See yuh later, Varron. Thanks for the drink."

"Don't mention it."

Hatfield touched Devlin on the arm, to say good-by.

"Where's he live?" he asked in a low voice.

"That big square adobe cattycorner across the plaza," Devlin replied. "Name's on the gate."

"Right."

Hatfield nodded and hit the batwings, which oscillated behind him. However, once outside, he paused and sought to strain the voices of Varron and Devlin from the general

45

murmur of the saloon.

"— he's all right, I tell yuh, Duke," Devlin was saying eagerly. "He's on the dodge, I'll swear to it!"

"Dry up," Varron snarled. "We'll talk later. I got to go now."

Chapter V:
Mystery

Jim Hatfield hustled away, walking with long strides over the plaza to the house which Devlin had indicated. There was a painted board with the name "Barry" on it, and he went rapidly to the porch. Two lighted windows were on his right, the door half open before him.

"Hullo!" he sang out. "Anybody home?"

"Come in, come in," called a high-pitched voice.

The tall man entered a narrow hall. The parlor door was wide and he looked in at a small, white-haired gentleman in a blue suit and white shirt with a string tie about his shriveled neck. The mayor who wore gold-rimmed spectacles was about seventy and spry in his movements. An old Frontier Model .44 Colt six-shooter that showed signs of much use hung in its worn holster from the peg in the wall.

"What can I do for yuh?" demanded

the oldster.

"Yuh're Mayor Jake Barry?"

"That's me," snapped the old fellow, peering through his thick lenses at the tall officer. "Say, they didn't spare the materials when they made you, did they?"

"No, sir. I reckon they must have had some left over and just throwed it in."

Barry laughed. "Yuh mean after gettin' through with me, huh? I ain't what yuh'd call large and I've sorta shrunk the past few years. Yuh're quick on the draw, ain't you? But hombre, I was just sittin' down to supper, and my Mex housekeeper gets mad if I ain't at the table on the dot, so mebbe —"

He broke off, licked his cracked lips. He was staring at the silver star set on a silver circle, the emblem of the Texas Rangers.

"Ranger, eh!" he muttered. "I wondered when you boys'd be in. McDowell sent yuh?"

"Yeah. Asked to be remembered. Says you and him are old trail pards. My name's Hatfield."

"Jim Hatfield, huh! I've heard tell of yuh, too."

"Let's not talk too loud," cautioned the Ranger. "I've come over on this range war, and I like to work quietlike till I've got everything straight, Mr. Barry. I've already give myself out as yore nephew, Jim Barry, to Duke Varron and his men."

"Huh." The little mayor looked alarmed. "I ain't got no nephew!"

Jim Hatfield laughed amusedly. "You have now and I'm it."

"All right," the little mayor gave in. "I'll say yuh're the son of a brother I thought died in the Montana gold rush. I did have one, but I ain't heard from him for thirty years."

"Senor Bar-ry!" an angry woman's voice called from the rear of the house. "Your dinn-air, she ees colder and colder!"

"That's Mercedes, my cook," said Barry. "I got one minute 'fore she comes after me with the skillet. Now look here. As to this range war. It's between Big Ed Lee and his rancher friends, and another bunch headed by an hombre named George Canty and that Duke Varron yuh mentioned. Canty was on trial for killin' Jack Lee, Ed's boy, but Varron and several others give him such an alibi the jury let Canty go.

"There's been gun duels and threats flyin' fast ever since. I ain't been able to get the straight of it, any more'n anybody else, but it's serious and growin' worse. Likely to end up in mass killin's. Lee's a good friend of mine but Canty's a neighbor in town, too, and I sorta make allowances for folks. Lee won't let the matter rest. He keeps threatenin' he'll get Canty and Varron."

"*Senor!*"

The cook's voice had a shrill insistence to it which started Barry hastily toward the closed door at the back of the parlor.

"Come eat with us," he said quickly. "There's a young lady here with me. I'll interduce yuh."

Hatfield had caught the pleasant odors of the meal. He was hungry and had been existing on cold rations for the past few days. He followed Barry into the dining room, in the center of which stood a square table with a white cloth on it, candles in shining holders, and silver utensils. A steaming dish of tamales and a platter of fried steaks stood waiting, while at the kitchen door was a huge, black-haired Mexican woman in a loose brown apron, scowling, her arms akimbo.

"Tamales don't wait," she snapped. "You eat."

"All right, Mercedes." Barry smiled at her. "Fetch another plate and fork. My nephew's just come."

"Your nephew!" She blinked at Hatfield, then her face broke into a broad smile. "Seet down, *caro mio,* seet down! What nice *muchacho, si!*" She vanished to bring more food.

"Doris," said Barry, "this here's Jim Barry, son of my long-lost brother. Jim, this is Ed Lee's girl."

Hatfield saw a small, exquisite girl step from the shadowed corner where she had been waiting. She had large violet eyes with long, curving lashes, and raven-black hair. When she smiled at the rugged Ranger, the full red lips parted on pearly teeth. Hatfield was struck by her loveliness. He bowed deeply.

"I'm happy to know you," Doris said, and he murmured an acknowledgement.

"Doris come to see me this evenin', Jim, my boy. But let's sit down and eat."

Hatfield jumped to help Miss Lee seat herself at the table.

"I got to tend my horse, Uncle Jake," he said. Then I'll be right back."

"Well, hurry it up or dinner'll be cold. There's a Mex stable boy out there — name's Pedro. He'll give yuh a hand."

Hatfield hustled back and picked up Goldy. He saw to it that the golden sorrel was unsaddled and rubbed down. The Mexican lad who worked for Barry was expert with animals and obviously loved them, and Hatfield let him take over.

He went back to the house and paused in the spacious kitchen. The smiling Mercedes brought him a basin of warm water and a bar of yellow soap. He washed up, and she was ready with a clean white towel.

"Nize boy," she said caressingly. "Go eat now. Mercedes like."

"Mille gracias," Hatfield said.

She spurted Spanish at him and the Ranger replied in the same language. His victory over her was complete when she found he spoke her native tongue.

When Hatfield went into the dining room Barry sat at the head of the table, Miss Lee at his right hand. Hatfield was starving, and the food was delicious. The cook kept bringing in tidbit after tidbit which she insisted Hatfield try. His appetite was keen and he did great justice to the warm meal. Barry and Doris were amused at the elderly Mercedes' mothering of the tall man.

"Yuh've shore made a ten-strike, Jim," Barry said laughing. "She bullies me, but she's babyin' you."

Mercedes, in fact, as Barry would gladly have admitted, took fine care of the bachelor Barry's home. She had worked for him for thirty years and was devoted to his interests.

They were eating a berry pie which had flaky, light crust and was the best Hatfield had ever tasted when there was a knock on the front door. Mercedes waddled to answer it, and came back, scowling.

"Eees Senor Canty. I say he mus' wait."

"George Canty!" exclaimed Barry, with a quick glance at Doris Lee, who put down her fork and rose quickly.

Jim Hatfield rose, too. He wanted a third helping of pie, but Doris excused herself.

"I can talk to him here, Jake," she said to the old mayor, and Barry nodded.

The mayor went to the connecting door and opened it. Hatfield, standing to one side so that he could be seen by anyone in the parlor, saw the burly man waiting there.

An icy finger touched the Ranger's flesh, as though some invisible, clammy hand had suddenly been laid upon him.

Keen, sensitive to impressions of character, he caught the calculation in the bright green eyes of the fellow in the parlor.

A blue shirt, open at the neck, could not hide the tremendous torso and bulging arm muscles of the mighty Canty. His wrists were wide and thick, his hands gnarled from handling iron and digging tools all his life. Yet his legs were slender compared to the overdeveloped body. He wore plain brown trousers and wide-toed brogans. He had removed his black hat, and the coarse, scanty red hair on his great head was awry. The freckles blotched his deep-burned face and Hatfield noted the straight, thin-lipped gash of the mouth, the determined set of the fighting jaw.

Strangely enough, Hatfield found that Canty kept eying him, after one quick look at Doris Lee and Mayor Barry.

"He's interested in me!" decided the Ranger. "Why?"

But Barry was doing the honors.

"Canty," Barry said, "Miss Doris come here, secret-like, to speak to yuh."

"I was going to visit you, Mr. Canty," said the girl humbly, "but perhaps we can talk here."

"Oh, yes, delighted — glad to talk," Canty replied, blinking at Hatfield. "Who's this young man, Barry? I ain't had the pleasure."

"This is my nephew, Jim Barry," replied the mayor. "He just pulled in. He's the son of my brother Martin, who was killed in Montana years back. I ain't seen Jim since he was a shaver, but he done took the trouble to look me up."

George Canty moved toward the Ranger, grinning so that his yellowed snags showed, a big hand shoved out. Now the officer realized what Canty had reminded him of, as the well-digger shuffled sideward, right shoulder down, over to him to shake. Canty gave the impression of a giant, dangerous crab.

"Glad to know yuh, Jim, my boy," Canty said and Hatfield felt the clamminess of the strange man's flesh as Canty pumped his arm.

"Good evenin', Canty," murmured Hatfield.

CHAPTER VI:
NIGHT INTRUDER

Hatfield felt the power of Canty's calculating eyes, sizing him up.

"Does he guess I'm a Ranger?" thought Hatfield. "Is that why he's so all-fired intrigued that he run over here?" For Canty was still puffing a bit from his run. "Mebbe Duke Varron told him I was in town. That's it — must be. Varron and Devlin knew it, and they're the only ones."

Yet Canty, as well as Big Ed Lee, had sent complaints to the Texas Rangers.

"Anyways, if he knew Lee had sent in," decided Hatfield, "it might be a smart play to complain hisself. Throw us off."

Mentally he girded himself, for the coming duel with George Canty. He glanced at Doris Lee. Her face was pale, but she held her head proudly. Then he saw she was trembling, and the white cambric handkerchief she gripped in her hand was bunched in a tight knot by her contracting fingers.

"She's afraid of him and fightin' it," he thought. "I don't blame her."

Canty was an insistent, unpleasant person who would not take no for an answer. He was hypersensitive on the other hand, quick to take offense and nurse a grudge. That was Hatfield's expert judgment of the crablike digger of wells in Pecosville.

As he studied Canty, he found Canty also was sizing him up, and dropped his lashes to hide any possible escaping give-away. He did not like Canty and he did not like the impression Canty gave. On the other hand, it was his duty to be fair, impartial, until he had made his investigation. A jury of his peers had acquitted Canty of murder.

"S'pose me'n Jim step out, and yuh can talk with Canty, Doris," suggested Mayor Barry.

"Yes, certainly," Canty nodded. He had a hoarse, deep-toned voice.

"Reckon I'll go outside and smoke a quirly, folks," Hatfield said.

He saluted Doris and Canty, and stepped through the front parlor door into the corridor.

Barry went back toward the kitchen. The street door was just ajar. Hatfield took out his tobacco and papers, and rolled a cigarette.

He hadn't meant to listen, but he could not help hearing Doris speaking in an earnest, pleading way.

". . . I do wish the trouble could be settled, Mr. Canty. I came to see you, secretly, because I so hoped you would help me. I don't want to see my father and my friends killed or injured, and I don't wish you to be hurt, either. Won't you call it off and stop this awful war?"

The appeal in her sweet voice was that of all women when confronted by war in which their loved ones were endangered. Canty's hoarse tones replied, as Hatfield listened.

"Miss Doris, I'm mighty glad to see yuh, and that goes for any and all times! Yuh're the prettiest girl I've ever seen and the sweetest. I'd do anything for yuh."

Canty's voice was caressing. Hatfield resented it, the way the man talked to the girl.

"Can that red-haired sidewinder figger she come to see him 'cause she *likes* him!" he muttered. "Is he that proud of hisself?"

"This war," Canty went on, "bothers me as much as it does you Miss Doris. I'd rather be friends with yore father. I never killed yore brother. Allison went off half-cocked when he accused me. I reckon his wound made him deelirious. Mebbe he seen someone with red hair and jumped to it that it was me. Now Duke Varron and others savvy there was a sorrel-topped outlaw lurkin' in them hills for a while, at the time yore brother was shot. He might've done it, and then run. I didn't touch Jack or Allison either. Like Varron and his men swore in court, I was miles away, with them, at the time yore brother died. It's yore father who's keepin' up this war, not me, Miss Doris."

"But Dad and Bob and some of the men say Varron's riders have fired on them with no provocation!" objected the troubled girl.

Canty laughed; an unpleasant sound.

"I happen to savvy that yore Dad's tryin' to catch Varron and his boys, and force 'em into talkin'. He thinks they'll change their stories, but he's wrong, for they told the truth on the stand."

"This don't help much," mused Hatfield.

He struck a match to touch it to his cigarette end. The porch door suddenly was pushed in, and Hatfield saw before him a brawny man with a bullet head too small for his powerful body, a man wearing a black patch over one eye and carrying a sawed-off shotgun in his blunt hands. He wore a black shirt, dirty corduroys, but no hat was on his matted, thick hair. Whiskers stuck from his chin and he scowled at the Ranger.

"What you doin' there?" he growled.

Hatfield regarded him coldly. "I might ask you the same thing," he replied. "I'd advise yuh to keep that shotgun muzzle down."

He grew alert, for the man with the patch on his eye was not alone. Two or three more men were in the porch shadows. Then Canty opened the side door, stuck out his head.

"What's wrong, One-Eye?" he demanded.

"Feller's standin' there listenin,' Boss," One-Eye replied.

"I was rollin' a smoke," Hatfield said deliberately. "Are these watchdogs yores, Canty? Tell 'em to lemme out. Or are we blocked?"

"Get outa here, yuh fools!" shouted Canty. He swung, apologized to Doris. " 'Scuse the language, ma'am. It's the only kind they understand."

One-Eye and his cronies retired to a corner of the porch, and Hatfield strolled out. The lamplights were glowing in the windows of Pecosville, and strains of a hurdy-gurdy came from the saloons.

"So he travels with a bodyguard," thought the Ranger, as he stretched his long legs on the plaza, smoking. "But that could be because of the war." Though cool as ice, Hatfield was inwardly excited by his contact with George Canty. "He's got power, one way or the other," he decided. "He's a stronger man than Lee or any others I've met so far. Ruthless, too, I'd say."

In his alert mind, he paraded those he had met since reaching the district. The explosive rancher chief, Big Ed Lee; the handsome, youthful Allison; Duke Varron, smooth, dangerous, but no equal of George Canty.

"I'm goin' to have sport here, I can see that," the Ranger mused. "I wish I savvied why he was so all-fired interested in me that he run to Barry's on the dot!"

He went back to the Prairie Fire Saloon, but Duke Varron, Devlin and the Lazy C were gone. After a drink, he strolled around, looking at the sights of Pecosville. At the southeast corner of the plaza stood a flat-roofed house with a high board fence around it. A sign was over the barred gate and he could read the big letters by the light of a street lamp:

GEORGE CANTY
Wells Dug, Piping and Iron-work

"So this is his den," he thought as, through

the iron bars of the heavy gate, he saw shadowed piles of equipment.

He rounded the plaza, and came through the dark alleyway, to the rear of Barry's home. The Mexican wrangler was lounging outside the stable.

"Nize horse, Senor." He grinned at the tall man.

Hatfield nodded and went inside, to look at Goldy. The gelding had been faithfully tended, and nuzzled his rider's hand, to say good night.

"I'm goin' to sleep under a roof for a change, Goldy, and so are you," Hatfield mumbled. "See yuh tomorrer."

He went in by the kitchen door and Mercedes hailed him joyfully. The remains of the pie stood on the table, and when she saw him glance at it, she seized his arm and made him sit down at the table, pouring him a glass of milk and dishing out the huge slice of pie. Hatfield consumed it, and passed a few amusing minutes speaking Spanish with the cook.

Canty was gone when Hatfield sauntered back to Barry and Doris Lee in the parlor. The girl's face was grave. There were tears in her eyes, tears she tried to force back.

"Canty said he'd do what he could," growled Barry, "so take it easy, Doris."

62

She shook her head. "I don't know what's the matter with me, Jake. I go around with the most horrible feeling of depression. It — it's as though I knew something awful would happen any moment."

Barry patted her gently. "That's 'cause of yore brother's death. Yuh'll get over it in time, my dear. Yuh better turn in and get a good sleep."

Mercedes took Doris to her room. Barry spoke for a time with the Ranger, in low tones, behind drawn blinds. Hatfield found the mayor somewhat confused over the situation in the district. Barry could add nothing to what the observant officer had already learned.

"I'm plumb wore out, Mr. Barry," Hatfield finally said. "Can I turn in?"

"Shore. A good idea. C'mon, I'll show yuh where yuh can stay while yuh're with me."

He lit a candle in a silver stick and, leading the way, took Hatfield to a second-story room overlooking the plaza. There was a large double bed, a washstand and a mat, chairs, some old prints, and a couple of books in the room. It was luxury to the Ranger, who was accustomed to sleeping on the ground with a saddle for a pillow.

Hatfield went to the window to open it, and could see the blinking lights of the

63

saloons on the other side of the street. Barry said good-night, the Ranger pulled off his boots and jacket, hung his gun-belt on the back of a chair close to his head, and blew out the candle. Stretching himself on the bed, he sank two feet into a deep feather bed.

But though he needed it, sleep wouldn't come. After a while he sat up, shaking his head.

"Dawg it I'm spoilt," he murmured. He lay down on the mat beside the bedstead. "This is better," he thought, and quickly feel asleep. . . .

Jim Hatfield woke with a start. His alert senses were at once fully alive, and against the faint stream of moonlight entering the open window, he saw a dark figure approaching. A board creaked faintly under the intruder's weight. He almost stepped on Hatfield's outstretched hand as he jumped to the bed and rammed the sawed-off shotgun he carried into its center. The covers, rumpled up by Hatfield's attempt to sleep in it, had fooled him.

"Get up and come along quiet —" he had begun to order in a husky whisper when, with a startled curse, he realized that the bed was empty.

Jim Hatfield was reaching for the Colt

.45s, depending in their supple holsters from the chair back a yard away. The intruder, his face a black blob, swung quickly, catching the slight rustle of the withdrawn revolver, for the movement was only a yard from him.

"Hold up, cuss yuh!" he rasped, and on the floor sighted the shadow of the Ranger.

"What's wrong?" a second man whispered from the open window.

The shotgun muzzles were whipping around to pin the officer. The Colt felt sweet to his long, slim hand, cocking under his thumb joint. He raised his thumb, aiming point-blank at the dark intruder in the room.

The shotgun roared an instant later, the unspread buckshot ripping into the floor mat, but Hatfield's slug did not miss. The masked fellow uttered a long-drawn-out screech and folded in a heap by the bed.

Hatfield glanced over his shoulder — another man was backing out through the door.

CHAPTER VII:
DANGEROUS WORK

"Murder! Thieves! Help!"

That shrill appeal came from across the upper hall, where Mayor Barry slept. Barry was yelling at the top of his lungs, and the answering screams of Doris Lee and old Mercedes rose in the night.

Hatfield was up on his knees, throwing bullets at the window. A flash came back at him, but the slug missed. Hatfield rushed out to answer Barry's call, bounded into the mayor's room. Barry was over by the wall and at the window, Hatfield saw a man's head and shoulders. They dropped out of sight as the Ranger raised his gun and fired at the marauder.

"That you, Jim?" shouted Barry.

"Yeah! What's goin' on?"

"I dunno. I heard them shots in yore room and jumped out of bed. A feller was slidin' in my winder and I run to get my Colt —"

Hatfield glided to the open window. He

66

heard running feet, but the intruders had swung close around the house and were not in his line of vision. He could see the moonlit plaza. Most of the saloons had closed, for it was after midnight.

Hurrying outside, then, Hatfield made a circuit of the place. A short ladder stood under his window, but the enemy had retreated and was hidden in the darkness. He paused at the stable, and heard a dull, thumping sound. Investigating, he discovered the Mexican boy, tied hand and foot and gagged, lying in an empty stall. The lad had been thumping with his bound feet on the wall.

Hatfield released him.

"Senor!" stammered the frightened youth. "I am sleep, but when I wake, I am tie!"

The Ranger swung toward Goldy's stall. His golden gelding was gone! Hatfield raced to the corral in the back but the sorrel was not there, either.

Angered at that discovery, the Ranger hustled into the house. Doris, Mercedes and the mayor were huddled together in the kitchen where the blinds had been drawn tight by the chattering, frightened Mexican woman. He lit a candle and, trailed by the mayor, went upstairs to his bedroom.

The man he had killed lay on the blood-soaked mat.

"Why," Barry cried sharply, as the candle rays touched the twisted face, "that's One-Eye Harry!"

"Works for Canty, don't he?" drawled the Ranger. It was the fellow who had stopped him at the door during the evening. "Hum — didn't lose no time tryin' for me!"

Was that because Canty knew he was a Ranger? But the marauders had gone after Barry, too. Had Hatfield not given the alarm, they would undoubtedly have killed the mayor.

He stooped, examining the body. Several short lengths of rawhide rope and a red bandanna were looped in One-Eye's belt.

"Why's he carryin' that stuff?" wondered Barry.

"Looks like he meant to tie and gag somebody," observed Hatfield. "Prob'ly me. The bed was rumpled up, like I was in it, and he rammed his gun into the middle and ordered me to get up and come along quiet!"

"I don't savvy it all," said Barry, shaking his head.

"I don't either — yet. Did yuh recognize the hombre in yore room?"

"No, it was too dark and I was het-up."

"Well, I'm goin' over and talk to Canty,

now," the Ranger announced, determinedly.

As Hatfield and Barry hurried across the plaza toward George Canty's, several citizens who had been awakened by the shouts and gunshots appeared, joining the party. In the lead, with his gun-belts on and Colts ready for action, Hatfield headed for the well-digger's home to have it out.

"Whose horse is that runnin' loose?" Barry called.

Hatfield heard the beat of hoofs, and his heart leaped with gladness as the golden sorrel ran to him, nuzzling his hand.

"Goldy! What happened to yuh!"

There was a rope halter on the sorrel, trailing after him. He was not harmed, as Hatfield saw, on swiftly examining him.

"That's a queer one," he thought. "Stealin' him, then lettin' him loose. Did yuh bust away, Goldy?" He wished his mount could talk, and tell him who had taken him from his stall.

Canty's house was dark and the gate was locked with a huge padlock. Hatfield, trailed by Barry and the curious townsmen, shouted and banged until a hoarse voice replied from the nearby window.

"Who the devil's that, this time of night?" Canty shouted angrily. "What yuh mean, bangin' a man out of bed like that!"

A gun was shoved through the black space of the window.

"Hold it, Canty," growled Hatfield. "It's the mayor and me — Jim Barry. We want to talk to yuh."

"Can't it wait till tomorrer?"

"No, it can't. Come out here and open up, 'fore I bust in yore gate."

"All right, all right. Keep yore shirt on."

Hatfield nudged Barry. "Take the lead," he said in his ear. "I'll put in my oar when it's needed."

Canty lighted a lamp in his main room. Then they heard the rattling of chain locks, and bolts. The huge, misshapen man came out, unlocked the gate, and they pushed inside. Canty rubbed sleep from his green eyes.

"Now what is it, boys?" he asked patiently.

There was nothing in sight to prove Canty had been out.

"Looka here, Canty," Barry began shrilly, "me'n Jim was near murdered in our sleep just now. Lucky Jim was sleepin' on the floor, 'cause he got a chance to shoot it out with a feller who tried for him. There was others, too, but they run. But the man Jim downed was One-Eye Harry, yore helper."

"What!" Canty jumped, began cursing furiously. His rage mounted, his face turning as red as a beet. "Why, that cursed lobo!" he stormed. "How dare he!" He leaped around in his fury, yelling: "Morg, Lefty, Tim! Come here, cuss yuh!"

At the doorway to the back of the place, three men appeared, carrying guns but without shoes or hats. They looked as though they had just jumped out of bed.

"What is it, Boss?" asked the thin one, his crooked nose twitching. At his elbow was a short, fat man, while the third was an oversized, adenoidal fellow with sandy hair and washed-out blue eyes.

"Have you boys been out?" snarled Canty.

"Huh?" answered Morg in an injured-innocent tone. "Why, no sir."

"What about One-Eye?" demanded the well-digger.

"We ain't seen him," chorused the trio.

"Not since early last evenin'," added Morg. "He was full as an owl, over at Dinty's, where his pards hang out. Wouldn't come home when we told him."

"G'wan, then, back to bed," snapped Canty. He turned back to Barry frowning. "That fool One-Eye never had no sense. Specially when he was full of red-eye, which was most of the time, gents. He must've cooked up a plan to rob yuh, Barry, with some shady pards of his. I was goin' to fire

One-Eye. He wasn't to be trusted. He got what he deserved." Canty sniffed, his eyes fixed on the little mayor. "I'm mighty regretful, Barry. I'd a drilled One-Eye myself if I'd had any idea what he was up to."

"Plumb pat," thought the Ranger, as he listened to Canty explain glibly, without a flicker of an eyelid.

Canty's men bore arms, as did the man they served. Beyond that, the shadows in the room were deep. And because there were heavy drapes, Hatfield wondered if unseen guns might be covering the party which had come to demand an explanation of Canty.

"Duke Varron might be around," he decided.

Intrigued by the well-digger and the whole set-up, and as yet unable to supply the answers to the many puzzles with which Canty presented him, Hatfield knew he must exert himself to the utmost in this hidden duel.

Barry accepted Canty's apology and explanation. There was little else he could do.

"Have a drink?" offered Canty. "No hard feelin's?"

Hatfield shook his head and slipped out the front door, where he stood looking over the yard. Stacks of rusting pipe, a crude derrick and some smaller machines, stood about. The high fence ran completely around the property.

Mayor Barry and the other Pecosville men came outside, and Hatfield walked with them across the plaza, leading Goldy.

"Well?" growled Barry, beside the Ranger. "What yuh think, Jim?"

"I think yuh better hire a couple of men yuh can trust, for night watchmen," advised the Ranger in his friend's ear. "Then we'll see."

George Canty stood at his gate grinning and waving, until Barry, Hatfield and the crowd had left. Then he locked the gate and went back inside, bolting the brown door after him. He turned the lamp down, and went to the rear of the parlor in which Barry, Hatfield and the others had been standing.

A heavy red portiere between two rooms hung to the floor. Canty pulled it aside, and nodded. Duke Varron crouched behind it, a double-barreled shotgun across his knees, and three of his aides, among them Devlin, the fellow whom Hatfield had helped, were close by him.

"They're gone," growled Canty. "It worked, Duke."

"I could've cut Barry and that big jigger

down easy as pie," Varron remarked.

"There were too many witnesses," declared Canty. "We'd have had to run for it, Duke, and that would have ruined our chances here." He shook his massive head, scowling.

"We need to keep our snouts reasonably clean," he went on. "I took a big chance tonight, sendin' my boys after Barry and that nephew of his. The feller is as fast as chain-lightin', seems like, and it was a narrow squeak for me. Lucky I was able to explain it as well as I did. It 'roused suspicions agin' me, however. Barry'll be leery of me from now on and he's got real power in this town. Owns most of it and folks like the old fool. I don't dare stick my neck out like that any more."

Duke Varron shrugged. "We done the best we could for yuh on the range, Canty. I can't go much further."

"Yeah, but drygulchin' and wild shootin' ain't shore enough, specially since Lee and his men are on guard. Oh, I ain't blamin' yuh. I made a mistake myself tonight — got excited when that Jim Barry showed up."

"On the other hand, we can't go on hopin' forever."

"No, we can't. Lee complained to the rangers, so I sent in a howl, after his'n, which is the way to confuse 'em. They'll be over here within a few days and we'll have to be more careful than ever with them snoopin' around. Sheriff Miles is busy in Redrock with that shootin' case, but anything big'll fetch him back here. What we do has to be done quiet — and I reckon I know what it'll be."

Varron licked his small black mustache.

"Lee, Allison, and Barry are still alive — and kickin'," he suggested.

"Add the mayor's nephew. We didn't count him in but he's got to die with them. Lee's rancher pards lean on him, and when he's done, they'll fade away. Any that don't will have to be taken care of, that's all."

"What about the young lady?" asked Varron. "Yuh started to tell me somethin' about her when we was interrupted."

A fatuous smile lighted the well-digger's ugly face. He blinked rapidly, and stroked his freckled jaw with a gnarled, hamlike paw.

"Yeah, Duke, she's a beauty! And by glory, I believe she'll have me, once her old man and that Allison ain't around to influence her. Yuh know what? She come to town, secret-like, to see me! I run over, when I got yore tip on Barry's nephew, and there she was, pretty as a pitcher, and just about to call on me! 'Oh, Mr. Canty,' she says,

75

'please don't hurt my dad. And I would hate to see anything happen to you!' That's what she said, or may I drop dead, Duke."

Varron guffawed, and slapped his chief on the back.

"Yuh old Romeo! She's a beauty, all right. Best-lookin' girl I ever see."

"She is. And that's another reason why I don't want to have her suspect anything, savvy? I figger she'll marry me like a shot soon as the way's clear."

His sensitive, evil ego inflated, George Canty had built himself a world, as yet imaginary, in which wealth, power and beauty were his. Then, he thought, people would no longer laugh at his queer appearance. Instead, they would kowtow to him as king of the range.

Though what he planned meant death and horror to those who stood in his way, Canty would charge ruthlessly through toward that goal.

CHAPTER VIII:
RANCHERS' PLAN

The great adobe ranchhouse of the Square L stood on the hill overlooking Horsehead Creek. At times, when the spring thaws melted the snows in the distant mountains, the creek flowed over its banks, but in summer and autumn it diminished to a trickle.

It was the chief water supply of the section, however, and Big Ed Lee's property flanked it for miles on both sides. Irrigation canals cut across his range carried the vital water to the adjoining ranches. And wells, dug by George Canty of Pecosville, before the range war had begun, supplemented the stream.

The golden sun beat down fiercely on the thick roof of the house, on the corrals, haybarns, stables and cribs, and a flat-roofed bunkhouse behind the *hacienda.* There were horses in the pens, and steers grazing over the range, steers branded with the various marks of the neighboring spreads.

Inside the spacious living-room, which had a stone open fireplace, Big Ed Lee faced a dozen Texans, his friends, and owners of adjoining ranches. There were Ollie Norton, of the Circle 1, a thick-set, quiet man of middle age, a second cousin of Lee's, who had followed the man across the Pecos twenty-five years before, to found the cattle empire. Next to Norton sat his two sons, and the Pruet men who ran the Cross 8.

The VV, Crooked T and Box Y finished out the brands represented. Their owners were middle-aged and grizzled, but their sons were fresh and strong from the outdoor life they led in the Texas sun.

Back at the various homes were the women — mothers and wives, grown daughters and smaller children, whose existences were bound up in these men. They were hard-working, honest folk who asked only to be let alone so they might fight with the forces of Nature for a living.

Big Ed Lee was their natural leader. Water and range were pooled, and he was ever ready to help a friend to the last two-bit piece he had in his jeans. In return, they looked up to him and loved him, and were behind him whenever he needed them.

The war between Canty and Duke Varron on one side, and themselves on the other, had disrupted this life for them. The range was no longer considered safe.

"I called yuh together, boys," Lee was saying to them, earnestly, "to tell yuh that yesterday afternoon one of Varron's gunnies, Ike Devlin, tried for us with a long-range rifle. He made a hole in my best hat. Allison rode him down, and we jigged him from a tree, tryin' to make him tell the truth about Varron and Canty. A stranger come along and horned in 'fore we could work Devlin out. It ain't the first time either, that I've been fired on, ridin' the range. Nor for Allison either. I thought I better warn yuh."

"Why don't we get together," suggested Norton, "and go clean out Varron's nest once and for all, Ed?"

Big Ed Lee shrugged. "I'll go. But seein' as it's all sprung from my affair, the killin' of my son —" He paused, his bulldog jaw setting. "Well, I ain't felt right about it. Varron's hired fifteen more tough riders since the Canty trial, no doubt 'cause he expects us to hit him. So they'll be ready for us, day or night, and that means we'll lose men. I hate to see my friends killed on my account."

Bob Allison lounged at the back of the room, listening to the elders confer. His left shoulder was still stiff, the flesh tight over the healed wound which had come close to puncturing his lung. A fraction of an inch had saved him from serious complications. Strength from good-living, and the tender nursing given him by Doris and her mother had brought him around. He was able to go about his work, although he was not quite as strong as he had been before Canty shot him.

Huge, broad-shouldered, and with his light hair cropped close to his handsome head now, and his brown eyes serious, he listened to the plan for the ranchers' attack on Varron's spread.

Allison had changed, somewhat, since the agony of his hurt. He knew what it felt like to have a chunk of lead half an inch wide tear through one's flesh. And he knew what it probably would mean for these friends of his to make a frontal attack on the Lazy C, Varron's den.

Big Ed Lee, when excited, would fight like a demon, but he was apt to be careless, too. All his friends were as brave as lions, and if they ran into a tough spot they would never retreat — but would die.

"Boss," Allison said earnestly, "if we do go after Varron, at least we ought to spy out the place first. As yuh say, Varron's hired some mighty tough-lookin' hombres lately."

"We'll show 'em who's tough," growled lean, dark-skinned Harry Young, of the Box Y. "I vote we ride up and clean that nest of skunks out pronto."

"Duke'll squawk and admit he lied on the stand for Canty, if we bust him," declared Norton.

"The main thing," Lee observed, "is to get George Canty. He's the killer, though Varron backs him. But if we break Varron, as yuh say, Ollie, we ought to be able to take Canty, too."

"What say we meet at my place at sundown Saturday?" suggested Sam Thomas. "It's nearest to the Lazy C, and we can start soon as it's dark. That'll give us three days to get our guns and hosses and men ready, and some of Duke's hombres are likely to be in town celebratin' over the week-end. Once we take the place, we can nab 'em as they come back."

"That's the stuff!" cried Norton.

Bob Allison heard them vote for this plan. He was as courageous as any other man, but he could see flaws in this scheme. They would lose heavily in such an attack, and might be defeated, crushed by Varron's gunnies.

He rose and strolled outside, to roll a quirly. Slim, young Val Norton, Ollie's second son, impatient at so much talk, trailed him out and borrowed "the makin's."

"Doris all right this mornin'?" inquired Allison casually.

"Huh?" said Val. "Why, I reckon so. You ought to know better'n me, Bob."

Allison looked puzzled. "Why, she's over at yore house, visitin' yore sister, Val. Didn't yuh see her 'fore yuh rode out?"

Val blinked. "Shucks, she must've been playin' hide-and-seek with me. I didn't see her, and nobody else mentioned her bein' there. When did she leave?"

"Yesterday afternoon, while we were out. She told her mother she was goin' to spend the night with you folks, and saddled up and rode off."

A pang of fear went through Allison's heart. What had happened to Doris? He went quickly inside, and inquired among the men there, but none had seen the girl. Confiding his fears to Big Ed Lee, Allison hurried to the corral, saddled up a fast mustang, and started out to trail Doris.

A mile out from the Square L, and well in advance of the others, worried over where the girl had gone, he topped one of the wavelike, grassy rises in the range, and his keen eyes saw two riders. A man and a woman were coming along the road to the

Lee home.

Relief flooded him as he dug in his spurs and spurted to meet them, for he had recognized Doris. The other rider was a man on a golden sorrel. In the excitement of seeing Doris and finding her unharmed — for he had imagined all sorts of things, a fall from her horse, with her lying injured all night in some cut, or even kidnaping at Varron's hands — he was almost upon the pair before it registered who the rider with Doris was.

"By the eternal, that's *him!*" he thought angrily, checking his mustang in a slide of dust.

For the tall rider with Doris was the man who had snatched Devlin from Lee and him the previous day.

"He's shore got his nerve with him!" Allison growled, the blood flushing his cheeks hotly.

He dropped his hand to his Colt butt, and walked his horse toward them as they came calmly on. The big man at Doris' side made no overt move, but simply eyed Allison.

"Doris!" shouted the outraged Allison. "What are you doin', ridin' with that sidewinder! He's a pard of Duke Varron's!"

She had been smiling at Allison, but her pretty face turned serious and she glanced quickly at the man beside her. Allison drew up six feet from them, his horse blocking the trail. The tall fellow on the handsome sorrel cocked a leg on his pommel and gravely watched the excited Allison.

"You're making a mistake, Bob," the girl said severely. "This is Jim Barry, Mayor Barry's nephew. He's a new friend of mine, and kindly escorted me from town."

Allison's breath left him in the excitement.

"Why — why — Doris! Yuh said yuh was goin' to Norton's!"

"I did not. I told Mother I might go there, but I changed my mind and went to see Mayor Barry. You mustn't act that way."

Women were beyond Allison. They were too quick mentally for him, and he found himself in the wrong, though he knew he had done nothing he shouldn't have done.

"I tell yuh this feller drawed a gun on yore Dad and me, Doris!" he blazed. "We had one of Varron's devils on a string and let him loose!"

"He explained it all to me," Doris replied, in an injured voice.

"Yeah, Allison," drawled the tall man, his gray-green eyes cool. Allison thought there was a hint of amusement in them at his discomfiture, too. "I'm mighty regretful about that. I'm a stranger here and was on my way to see my Uncle Jake. I come on some fellers stringin' another one up and it surprised me. I went off half-cocked, I reckon, and I'm sorry."

Allison scowled. He was a fair-minded man, as a rule, but the set-up annoyed him. A bit of jealousy, for the tall man was striking in appearance, tinged his mind, already disturbed by worry. Then astonishment and the rebuke his sweetheart had administered put a finishing touch to his discomfiture.

He shrugged. Violence was out of the question, so far as he was concerned. Doris had Jim Barry tamed, and Allison could not shoot a man who was apologizing. "All right," he growled to the girl. "You can go explain to yore dad about this feller and where yuh was, Doris. I got work to do."

Doris started her horse and rode past him without another word. Allison sat his saddle, watching the two as the tall man gravely saluted him and trailed the girl.

"Well, doggone it," fumed Allison. "What did I do that I shouldn't?"

Chapter IX:
A Call on the Lazy C

Allison swung southeast across the rolling plain, studded with mesquite and bunch grass, and with red buttes thrusting to the brassy sky here and there. The day was hot but Allison was inured to the sun. He rode fast, thinking things over.

A few miles to his right was the spot where Jake Lee had died, and Allison had been wounded. He veered off from it, and found himself on a trail running along a ridge. It led to Duke Varron's eventually.

"By glory, I'm goin' over and take a look," he decided. "If Lee and the boys hit there Saturday, somebody ought to spy it out first."

Action was what he craved, and danger, too, to soothe his ruffled emotions. A lover's quarrel is not too serious, but it is nonetheless serious enough to the participants at the time.

Late in the afternoon, Bob Allison left his

horse at the foot of a steep cliff and climbed slowly to an eyrie from which he knew he could observe Duke Varron's home. It was a hard climb and Allison was puffing and sweated when he reached the peak and lay flat, looking out over a breath-taking dip. Below him was the Lazy C.

"I'd like to get my hands on that Varron swine," he muttered. "I'd make him talk."

But Varron was careful. He never moved far from home without a large guard of tough fighting men.

Allison could make out the figures of men in the side yard of the spread now. The shadows were lengthening, spreading far across the flats below.

"I believe that's Varron," Allison decided, as a figure, familiar even at such a distance, moved across the yard and went into the front door of the house.

Bob Allison had a strong feeling of opposition to Big Ed Lee's projected attack on Varron's stronghold. The road to it was guarded, he was certain, and he had a hunch as well that it might prove a costly failure to his friends.

"If I could grab Varron, that might settle the whole business," he muttered. "Wonder if I could get down that cliff in the dark?"

He might do it with a rope, he decided. It

would be perilous but then he would be close to the buildings and could approach from an unexpected angle.

Returning to his horse, he threw his lariat over his shoulder and climbed back up to the crest. He spent the remaining hours of daylight in picking a route down the steep red rock wall on Varron's side of the ridge.

As soon as dark came, Allison began the descent. Boots left behind, for the heavy leather and spurs would impede him, he felt for the footholds he had picked, the rope helping him to make the drops. It took him over an hour, but then he found himself in the blackness, beneath the towering bluffs. A lamp burned in Varron's front room, and Allison stole toward the place, excited by his success so far.

He had his plan worked out, a bold, but basically simple scheme to escape with Varron.

Foot by foot, keeping low and taking advantage of the shadows, Bob Allison crept up on the Lazy C ranchhouse. The lighted windows were beacons in the night. He circled to the side away from the corral and barn, and on knees and hands he drew in bit by bit, pausing now and then to listen carefully.

The window was open. Through it Allison

peeked inside the room. The unpainted wooden wall was black in the shadow.

Duke Varron lay sprawled on a bunk on the other side of the main room. He had a bottle by him which he kept lifting with regularity.

"Now or never," thought Allison, and drawing his Colt, he pulled himself up and vaulted inside.

Leveling the pistol on Varron, just across the floor from him, Allison ordered in a low, terse voice:

"Keep shut, now, Varron, or yuh die! I ain't foolin'! Get up and come along with me."

Varron's shifty black eyes widened with sudden terror. He choked, then began to shake.

"Don't — shoot!" he begged.

"Stand up, and do as I say, or yuh'll eat lead! Savvy? Keep yore hands where I can see 'em."

Varron's gun-belt hung from a chair back out of reach, so he rose quickly.

"What now?" he demanded, tense with fear of death.

"Call out that window and tell yore wrangler to fetch two saddled mustangs, fastest yuh got, to the front door."

Varron walked carefully to the opening as

directed.

"Hey, Tiny!" he called. "Slap hulls on them two fast chestnuts in the stable and fetch 'em to the front for me. Pronto."

"All right, boss," a voice sang back.

Allison, Colt up, turned the lamp down with his left hand.

"Stand by the door, Duke," he commanded. "Remember, if yore men try for me, yuh die!"

Varron gulped. "I'll remember."

He could see Allison's big thumb on the Colt hammer. All it had to do was rise and Varron would be killed. In a pinch like this, Duke Varron was afraid. He dared not make any move to get Allison.

Minutes that dragged like hours to Allison passed by. At last the wrangler's voice sang out again from the front:

"Here yuh are, Duke, all set."

"Outside, and mighty careful," growled Allison, approaching the most ticklish point of his planned escape with Varron under the gun.

He stood behind Duke, just out of reach in case Varron tried to whirl. Duke stepped out on the creaking boards of the veranda, and before them in the faint moonlight were two sleek-limbed blacks, fast mustangs with an Arab strain in them. One of Duke's men was holding the reins. He didn't recognize who was behind his boss, as Duke mounted the first horse.

Allison hit leather without descending to the ground, jumping aboard in a mighty spring.

"Get goin'!" he cried, but then something coiled about him from above, tangling his arms.

There was a hard jerk as he fought. The black began bucking under him and even his iron knee-grip couldn't hold as he was pulled inexorably out of his saddle.

"Attaboy!" Duke Varron yelled in sudden hopeful joy. "Get him, men!"

Heavy bodies leaped from the low-hanging porch roof onto the stunned Allison, beating him to earth, wresting from him the wildly discharged pistol. He fought them with all his terrific strength, but more and more rushed up to fall upon him.

Booted feet kicked the wind out of him, and his face was cut and slashed. Gun butts rapped his skull and at last, breath gone, and tangled in the lariat, Allison lay still.

"Fetch him in here," Duke Varron snarled.

Varron turned up the lamp, and the rays showed the blood pouring from Allison's cheeks and temple, the dirt ground into him, the torn clothes. But he held himself proudly, as Varron scowled, facing him.

"Lucky I happened to be in the kitchen and heard him, Boss," chortled Devlin.

He it was who had been on the porch roof with the rope and a couple of other gunmen and dropped on Allison from there, in order to save Varron.

Varron swore and hit Allison in the mouth with his fist.

"Tables turn, don't they?" he gloated.

CHAPTER X:
A RANGER BADGE

Not mentioning the short encounter with Bob Allison, Jim Hatfield escorted Doris Lee toward her home. He had, as he had repeated to Allison, told her about the "mistake" he had made, in saving Devlin from her father. He had explained it easily enough, since she was prejudiced in his favor. Impressed at how he had saved Mayor Barry and by his strong personality, Doris had become his firm ally.

"Father's an excitable man, Mr. Barry," warned the girl, "but I'm sure we can bring him around."

In nothing the play between the girl and young Allison, Hatfield had read that the two were deeply in love. Little quarrels did occur between sweethearts, and Allison's confusion at Doris' attitude had secretly amused Hatfield, who kept a solemn face, however.

She rode on with the Ranger toward the

ranch, and soon they met two cowboys whirling along at full-tilt. They pulled up.

"Miss Doris! Yuh all right? Yore dad and the rest were just startin' to hunt yuh!"

"Go on back and tell them I'm fine and I'll be there in a few minutes," she ordered, and the waddies whipped off.

Reaching the gates, she remarked:

"There's a meeting, I guess. That's how Bob found out I wasn't at the Nortons'. You wait out here, Mr. Barry, till I can speak to Father. Suppose you go over to the barn, and I'll fetch him there."

"*Bueno*. I'd like to talk to him alone."

He watched her turn toward the big ranchhouse, then he swung the sorrel to the great barn two hundred yards away, and left Goldy on the far side, in the shade. An open door let him inside the barn and he rolled a quirly, smoking as he waited for Doris to bring out her father.

It was only a few minutes until he heard the heavy tread of the giant rancher. The girl was talking to him as they approached. Hatfield looked from a square window and watched Big Ed and his daughter coming to the barn. He could hear what they said.

"Father, you *must* understand! This man is a friend, not an enemy."

"Yeah, but yuh haven't told me yet who

94

he is," Lee objected.

"He'll tell you himself, and I'll be there to guarantee it," Doris declared. "Please, now! Don't fly off the handle."

"Who, me? Why, Baby, I don't never lose my temper, you savvy that!"

She smiled and patted his arm affectionately. Hatfield leaned against the wall near the door, the cigarette sending a curl of gray smoke from his lips. Big Ed Lee and Doris came in at the front and Lee stopped short, his eyes growing accustomed to the dimmer light inside the barn.

"Howdy," he said, seeing the tall figure in the shadow.

"This is Jim Barry, Dad," said Doris. "He's Mayor Barry's nephew, and he was on his way to visit Uncle Jake in Pecosville when he —"

Lee uttered a sudden roar as his eyes widened. Now he could clearly see the features of the fellow Doris had brought him to meet.

"You!" he bawled, his huge paw flying to his six-shooter. "You! Got the nerve to come here and —"

He whipped up his Colt, leveling it at the Ranger who stood coolly watching him.

"Hold it, Lee," Hatfield drawled. "I made a mistake, mebbe, in snatchin' Ike Devlin from yuh. On the other hand, mebbe it was a favor. When yuh take the law into yore hands, yuh have to answer to the law for it."

"Why, curse yore hide! I got a mind to drill yuh!"

"Dad, stop it!" ordered Doris indignantly. "You promised you'd control yourself. Put that Colt back where it belongs!" She stepped in front of her father's gun, shielding Hatfield. "I tell you, this is the mayor's nephew, a friend. He's apologized. And last night he saved Uncle Jake's life when some marauders attacked the house. He's a fine man and a good one —"

"Get out of the way, Doris. I'll . . . Shucks, he threw in with Devlin, who's one of Duke Varron's killers."

Lee's face was red with fury. But under the girl's persuasion, he slid his gun back into its case.

"All right," he growled, more quietly. "But I ain't shakin' hands with him. I don't forget as easy as all that!"

"S'pose," suggested Hatfield easily to Doris, "that yuh let yore father and me have a talk together?"

"All right," Doris said hesitantly. "Behave yourself, now, Dad. Remember, Jim Barry is my friend."

Big Ed Lee looked sour. The girl smiled at

Hatfield and left the two in the barn.

"Well?" snarled Lee. "Say whatever yuh got to, feller. It won't change my mind none."

Hatfield held up his right hand. Cupped in it was the Ranger emblem, the silver star on silver circle, known throughout Texas as the badge of the bravest and fairest fighting police in the world. Lee's eyes popped and his chin fell.

"Well, for . . . Why in tarnation didn't yuh say so!" he gasped.

"I like to get a line on things, when I hit a new neighborhood, Lee," replied Hatfield. "Yuh see, when I ran into three hombres stringin' up a fourth, I had to do my duty."

"We wouldn't have killed him. Only meant to dance him a while and see if he'd squawk. Yuh savvy what's goin' on here?"

Hatfield nodded. "That's why I was sent to Pecosville, Lee — to rake over these coals and see what's what. Canty and you are runnin' a war. Yore son was shot, and Allison accuses Canty. Duke Varron is Canty's man."

"And since Jack died," Lee added, "two of my friends have been nicked by drygulcher slugs. I'm shore it's Canty, eggin' Varron on. They've fetched in a bunch of gunnies and it's growin' worse by the minute. I'm determined to bust Canty, and make Varron admit he lied on the witness stand when he give Canty an alibi provin' Canty wasn't where Allison said he was."

"What started it all?"

"Why, Canty gunned my son and Allison. Ain't that enough?"

"Enough for you. But why did Canty begin?"

"Canty dug all the wells in this district, Ranger. But he charged me too much and cheated me. So I told my boy Jack and Allison to take a gang of Mexes and put down one — water's scarce. Canty come along, got sore 'cause we hadn't hired him, and rode off, after some words with the boys. But he sneaked back and dry gulched 'em. We'd never have knowed who done it, but Allison wasn't killed, and he had spied Canty behind a butte from which Canty was firin'. Allison got well. That was him yuh seen me with the day yuh saved Ike Devlin. The big feller with the light hair. He's like a son to me, and him and Doris, my daughter, are engaged."

The Ranger star, showing Hatfield's official position, had changed everything. For when Lee had sent for help to Austin, he had hoped such an officer as Hatfield would come to settle the feud.

"Me and my friends will throw in our guns with yuh, Ranger," Lee promised. "We're plannin' to hit Varron's spread, the Lazy C, which is three hours run southeast of here, on Saturday. We mean to get the truth outa that Duke son."

Hatfield shook his head. "It don't sound too good, Lee. From what I hear, Varron's got plenty of gunnies with him. No doubt they'll be watchin' for just what yuh're plannin'. I'd advise yuh to wait till we're better set and know what's what."

"Well, the boys are all determined to have it out — and pronto. They're inside, now . . . Say, does Doris know yuh're a Ranger?"

"No, and I haven't told anybody here except Jake Barry. I'm s'posed to be his long-lost nephew, till I can get a line on things. I'd rather you kept this to yoreself, 'bout me bein' a Ranger. I met Allison just now on the trail, and he was mighty upset at seein' me. He rode on. Who was that other waddy with yuh the day we first met?"

"That was Paul Winters, one of my riders," replied Big Ed Lee. "He's out, now workin'. I'll tell him to keep his trap shut if he sees yuh."

"*Bueno.* From what I've learned already, George Canty's a tough customer, Lee. I'm here to help yuh, and yuh're to run things as I say. *Sabe?*"

Lee's strong eyes drilled into the cool, gray-green depths of Hatfield's. He thrust out his great hand, growling:

"Right, Ranger. I'm yore man."

"S'pose we go in, and let me meet yore friends, so I'll know 'em. Introduce me as Barry's nephew."

Hatfield followed the huge rancher to the house, and Lee did the honors.

"Boys, this is Jim Barry, a nephew of our friend Jake's. He's come to visit us, and he's all wool and a yard wide. Yuh have my word for it."

Hatfield shook hands with the cowmen. They were decent, honest Texans, and he liked them. His magnetism attracted them, and Lee's recommendation made him at once welcome. Mrs. Lee and Doris served up a snack for the men, and Hatfield partook of it. He talked with some of the ranchers, seeking a possible motive for the war.

"Canty," he mused as he listened, "had no reason for killin' young Lee and Allison, beyond rage at losin' a two-bit job! Would he put his head in a noose for that?"

Canty might, he decided, from injured pride. He had sized the well-digger up and knew that Canty had a swollen ego and a hypersensitive skin.

"After that trial, though," he thought, "why did he keep it up? Simply to devil Lee and his friends?"

It was an elaborate set-up, and a perilous one for Canty and Varron, to run such a war with personal satisfaction at bedevilment the only reason for it. And, the Ranger asked himself, what was the meaning of the attack on Mayor Barry and himself? Where did it fit into the general picture of Canty versus Lee?

Big Ed was Hatfield's firm ally now, though, and would direct his fighters as the Ranger desired. Hatfield did not tell Lee to call off the mobilization for the week-end. For if the situation warranted it, he might use the ranchers against the powerful enemies he was ferreting out.

The afternoon was running out. Lee's neighbors had work to do, and, the conference over, they split up and mounted, starting home. Big Ed went out to the west pasture with several of his hands, and the Ranger was left at the house with Doris and her mother. He found the girl standing outside, at the end of the long veranda. She was watching the road to Pecosville, along which Hatfield and she had come.

"I wonder where Bob went," she said, as she smiled at Hatfield. "He was angry, wasn't he?"

"Yes'm. But he'll soon get over it," he replied softly. "I reckon I'll ride around some and look over the country."

CHAPTER XI:
MESSENGER OF DEATH

On the golden sorrel, Hatfield ranged over the rolling, thickgrassed plains. From a height, he saw how the little creek, controlled by Big Ed Lee, irrigated the pastures and furnished water for stock to the several ranches of the vicinity.

"Why, Lee could cut off Pecosville if he'd a mind to," he thought. "Wonder if Canty's after the water?" He shook his head. "That's all right, as far as it goes, but it don't explain Canty's attempt on the mayor and me last night."

At sundown he returned to the Square L. Big Ed Lee was in, the waddies were waiting for the supper, the appetizing odors of which were in the clean, tangy Trans-Pecos air. But Bob Allison had not showed up, and Doris was worried.

"It isn't like Bob to stay mad this way," she told the Ranger anxiously. "I hope nothing's gone wrong."

"Oh, he'll be along," comforted Big Ed Lee.

But suppertime came and went, and bedtime arrived without Allison appearing.

"Mebbe he took a run into town," suggested Hatfield, "or rode to a neighbor's."

They admitted that might be a possibility, but no one was entirely satisfied when finally they turned in.

Hatfield woke early, and found Doris and her mother in the kitchen.

"I hardly slept a wink," the girl told the tall man. "I kept listening for Bob to come in."

Hatfield began to feel uneasiness himself, for he realized that the range and Pecosville were not safe for an enemy of George Canty's. When he had eaten breakfast and taken his leave of the Lees, he knew that Big Ed also was troubled. He had ordered his men to saddle up and start hunting Allison.

The Lazy C, Varron's spread, was southeast of Lee's Square L. It was not on the road to Pecosville but the trail cut across the route farther down, the shortest way being to ride over Lee's south range.

"I reckon I'll take a peek at Varron's, anyways, 'fore I go back to Canty," the Ranger decided, as he rode swiftly from the Square L.

The sun was not yet up, but its red glow was streaking the horizon to his left as he moved on. It came up as he rode in the exhilarating, keen air, a red ball, turning to yellow. It was around nine A.M. when he sighted smoke far to his left, and some tall ridges. Then, from a crest, he sighted a dust column headed his way.

He drew back, dismounted, and waited. A faint sound, carried on the breeze, came from the other side, toward the smoke. Glancing that way, he saw four horsemen appear from behind some thick mesquite and head toward the broken formations above. They came quite near Hatfield, hurrying in answer to the hails of a fifth man who suddenly broke into the Ranger's view from back of the steep-rising ground.

"Hey, boys, I found it!" Hatfield heard this fifth sing out.

He rode a chestnut mustang, and was leading a saddled animal behind him, a riderless horse.

"Couple of them are Varron's men — I seen 'em in town," decided Hatfield. "Reckon the rest are, too."

Then he started. He had recognized the mustang with the empty saddle.

"Allison's!" he muttered. "He was ridin' that black-and-white when Doris and me met him yesterday! They've got him. The young fool must've gone in and got caught!"

He feared that Allison might already be dead. From what he had learned, Varron and Canty wanted the young fellow killed.

"It would shore break that girl's heart," he thought.

The quintet of heavily armed Varron gunnies, rifles gleaming in their boots, double Colts sagging their shoulders with the laden cartridge belts crossed over their bodies, stopped and looked at the black-and-white mustang. Then they turned and rode swiftly back toward the plume of cook-smoke marking the Lazy C.

Hatfield frowned. In the excitement of seeing Allison's animal he had forgotten the rider coming from the direction of Pecosville. Glancing that way, he saw the fellow, pounding swiftly on a lathered bay toward the Lazy C.

"Ike Devlin!" he exclaimed.

Mounting, the Ranger cut down, keeping the slanting ridge crest between Devlin and himself, and pulled up in some mesquite lining the trail.

He was just in time. Devlin was a hundred yards to his right and flogging hard, his sharp nose pointed for home.

Hatfield shoved the golden sorrel out into the path. Devlin's shifty black eyes widened with alarm but then he recognized the tall fellow. He pulled to a sliding stop, for Goldy and his rider blocked the way.

"Why, howdy, Jim! Out early, ain't yuh?"

"Same to you, Ike. Where yuh bound in such a sweat?"

"Oh — I'm goin' to the ranch. Been in town."

The dark eyes glanced off as Hatfield fixed them. Devlin didn't want to look at him, and he was uncomfortable under the tall officer's scrutiny. Ike shook his round head that was capped by a loose-fitting black Stetson held on by a chinstrap. He wore two Colts, and a carbine rode the leather boot under one stringy leg, while his fat belly pushed against the slant of the pommel.

"I've been huntin' yuh, Ike," explained Hatfield.

"Yeah? That right?"

"Yeah. I'm gettin' bored, Ike, I need some excitement. Uncle Jake, the old skinflint, is lined with *dinero*. But he won't part with it. I been figgerin' how to ease it out of him."

Devlin blinked. He did not take the bait as he should have. There was a blank wall now between him and the man who had saved him from the rope, and Hatfield sensed it.

"I thought yuh were a pal of mine, Ike," the Ranger said aggrievedly.

"I — I got to get in, Jim," said Devlin, trying to shove past him.

"What's yore all-fired hurry?" snapped Hatfield, scowling.

Devlin had seen the big fellow in action, against the Square L men. He was too aware of Hatfield's terrific speed to try a draw, and he knew a bluff would not work, either. He gulped. Hatfield had saved him, but on the other hand, he had his orders. His chief —

"Aw, look, Jim, I'm takin' a message to Duke and I got to make it pronto." He patted his breast pocket.

Hatfield's horse, across the trail, blocked him off.

"Reckon I'll ride in and talk to Duke myself. Mebbe he'll give me a job."

Devlin came to his decision. He was condemning the tall man to death and he knew it, but business was business. He would be rewarded for luring Jim Barry into a trap.

"All right — come on," Devlin agreed.

As he found Hatfield pulling back to let him take the lead, Devlin started. But as he came close, a steel hand reached out and seized his wrist.

"I don't like the way yuh behave," snarled Hatfield, in his role as a bad actor, the renegade nephew of Mayor Barry. "Let's see that note yuh got in yore pocket."

Devlin felt the strength of the long fingers and his eyes popped.

"No — cut it out, now, Jim. I ain't lookin' for trouble, but —" He gave a yip of anguish as the vise cracked his arm. "Leggo! Yuh're killin' me. . . . Oh, all right, take it!"

Hatfield eased his hold, and seized a folded sheet of dirty white paper from Devlin's pocket. Facing Devlin, he quickly glanced at the message, printed in pencil. The hurried scrawl read:

If you find his horse, and are sure he wasn't trailed to the ranch, finish him off and destroy all evidence. If there's any doubt, hold him till you hear again from me.

There was no salutation and no signature, but Hatfield was certain it was from George Canty and that it concerned Allison.

"At least they haven't polished him off yet," he mused, his stern eyes pinning Devlin.

"Yuh got yore nerve with yuh," growled the gunny. "Yuh —"

"Dry up! One move out of you, and I'll make yuh coyote bait. Savvy?"

He had to save Allison, no matter what. A frontal attack, by the Square L, might result in Duke Varron's killing Allison before they could get in — if they got in.

"That message is from Canty to Varron, ain't it?" he said to Devlin.

Ike Devlin shrugged. Dark blood flushed his pockmarked cheeks.

"Yuh better not fool around with us, Jim," he warned. "Yuh saved me, mebbe, but yuh're goin' too far —"

"Shut up, I said."

Hatfield's hand caught the fat-bellied lieutenant of Canty by the throat, and again Devlin felt the strength of the tall man. His eyes bulged and his tongue came out. Pressed together, the mustang gave way as the powerful Goldy pushed against Devlin's mount.

"From here on yuh do exactly as I tell yuh, Devlin," the Ranger growled, "or yuh die, savvy? I'll be right by yuh and I can kill yuh before yuh can wink. I'll make a point of gettin' yuh, even if they down me. I can do it. First we'll ride and pick up some friends. Then we're goin' in to the Lazy C.

Yuh'll hand Duke Varron the note I give yuh, instead of the one Canty wrote. And if yuh try to slip away from me or make the slightest sign of warnin', yuh're dead."

Devlin was frozen to his saddle. He kept his hands on the horn, watching with deep-seated fear as Hatfield took a pencil and piece of paper from his pouch and began to write. Facing Devlin from the steady sorrel's back, Hatfield could see his prisoner as he worked.

It took him no more than a minute to imitate Canty's printed scrawl. As he completed the message, the sound of hoofbeats came from around the turn toward the Lazy C, and by Devlin's sudden look of hope, the Ranger guessed it must be friends of his captive's.

He hastily folded the paper and stuffed it into Devlin's pocket. Swinging Goldy, he whispered in Devlin's ear:

"Remember!"

The two were riding slowly along together as half a dozen riders with the Lazy C brand on their mustangs swung up to them, hands on guns.

"Hey, Ike!" the bearded leader cried. "So yuh're back! Who's that with yuh. . . . Why, say, if it ain't Jim Barry!"

"Hullo, gents," Hatfield said easily. "Met

111

Ike in town and we're goin' to see Duke. I got some business to talk with yore boss."

The Varron men stared at Hatfield. He had the same impression that had come when Devlin looked at him, that they believed they were face-to-face with a condemned person, someone still alive but who would not be for long.

Devlin was on tenterhooks; Hatfield was just behind him, and the round-headed gunny remembered the promise that he would be first to die. He was afraid that these men would try to take the tall man.

"We got to hustle, Lefty," he said quickly, gruffly. "Duke's waitin'."

Lefty and his men pulled to one side. Eyes blinked, dropped from Hatfield's gray-green gaze as he went past.

Following Devlin, Hatfield rode the trail to the Lazy C. The men with Lefty swung and tagged along behind, at a hundred-yard interval, talking among themselves. Their sudden appearance had prevented Hatfield from hurrying back, with Devlin in tow, to contact Lee and have reserves waiting, at least within a mile or two of the Square L. He had plunged into it alone and now it was life or death, not only for Allison but for himself.

The trail, as they drew closer in to the

Lazy C, was well-guarded by nests of hidden sentries. They were challenged four times within half a mile, at turns and rocks by the wayside.

Devlin provided the password. Hard eyes focused on Hatfield, riding just back of Ike, as the Ranger coolly headed straight into the jaws of death on Bob Allison's track.

CHAPTER XII:
ENEMY CAMP

Sweat beads stood out on Devlin's dirty brow, and rolled down his bearded cheeks as he led Hatfield into the Lazy C yard. There stood the house, raw, ugly and run-down, all its flaws plainly visible in the brilliant sunlight. A few scrawny pines grew near. Five hundred yards in the rear were some thick woods, and on the south broken rocks rose to a high ridge that curved westward and formed the palisades over which the unfortunate Allison had come.

Hatfield swiftly took in the strategic strength of Varron's ranch as a stronghold. The only way a large body of riders could get in, fast, was up the main trail, and that would mean ambush and wholesale death if the road was defended. Tough, armed fighting men were in sight, Lazy C riders and new gunmen Duke had been taking on.

Duke Varron saw them from inside, through the open window, and recognized

Hatfield. Leaping up, he hustled out as Devlin and the tall man dismounted. Varron came down the steps, stroking his ridiculous little black mustache. He was excited, inwardly, at sight of Mayor Barry's nephew.

He jumped to the conclusion that Devlin had pulled off a clever coup, in leading one of their star victims into the lion's jaws.

"Well, well, howdy, Barry! Hullo, Ike."

Devlin sniffed. His body was tense. He gingerly reached in and passed the note to Varron.

Duke unfolded it quickly and scanned it. He read what Hatfield had prepared:

Turn him over to Devlin and Barry. They'll fetch him here. Jim's with us. Trust him. See you later.

Varron's mustache twitched and his black eyes rolled in astonishment.

"Well, for —" he snapped.

Looking up, he scowled at Hatfield, then at Ike Devlin.

Quite a crowd had gathered on the porch and others were circling them. Wolf-eyed men waited, expecting to see the tall, imperturbable fellow they knew as "Jim Barry" either cut down or taken prisoner. Hatfield, weight on left leg, and long, slim

115

hands hanging easily close to the heavy Colts in their supple holsters, was ready. Ike Devlin knew it, and knew that he would be the first to feel the murderous lead from those guns.

"Get the devil out of here!" snarled Duke Varron, waving the curious onlookers off.

They scattered, heading back to the shade, to their drinking or card games. Varron crunched up the paper in his hand, deeply puzzled by Canty's message. It did not jibe with what he had last agreed on with the chief. Still, time had gone by since then and, in such an affair, matters might rapidly change.

Duke scratched his greased, slick black hair, and said to Devlin:

"Canty told yuh to give me this, huh, after yuh handed him my message?"

"Shore as guns," replied Devlin.

His voice broke into falsetto, and he drew in a quick breath. Sudden death was beside him and he had been with it for an hour that had dragged like eternity. He was acutely aware of the towering man so near him.

"What's wrong with yuh?" demanded Duke Varron. "Yuh're white as a sheet, Ike."

"It's mighty, hot ridin', that's all," Ike replied quickly, with an involuntary glance at the Ranger.

"H'm. I don't savvy this at all." Varron scowled at Hatfield.

Hatfield was ready — ready for a fight to the finish if it came to that. He was taking a bold chance, but he counted on Ike Devlin's spirit of self-preservation to help him through. Duke Varron suddenly swung on his high-heeled boots and went over to the open window at the side of the house.

"Tiny!" he bellowed. "Come here!"

Hatfield, leaning against the porch pillar not far from Devlin, could see "Tiny" hurrying at his boss's shout. Tiny was the opposite of his name, fat and huge, with a double chin and a round stomach that shoved at his gun-belts.

"Bring Allison in here, Tiny. And I want twenty men ready to go in fifteen minutes."

"All right, Duke." Tiny waddled off toward the low-roofed stable.

"Help yoreselves to a drink," Varron said, waving at the table in the back.

He straightened out the letter, and again stared at it, shaking his sleek head and pulling at a sideburn with his free hand.

"Come on, Ike, yuh need a drink," said the Ranger, shoving the tense Devlin toward the table. "Yuh can pour me one, too."

"What now?" whispered Devlin hoarsely.

His hand shook as he raised the tumbler to his dry lips.

"Keep a stiff upper lip," the Ranger said in an undertone that could not reach Varron. "Once we get Allison out of here, I'm goin' to turn yuh loose. But remember, if anything goes sour —"

"S'pose it ain't my fault?"

"Ssh — Keep it shut!"

Varron had started toward them, but had paused, then gone back to the front door.

"Fetch him in here," Hatfield heard him say.

Hatfield poked Devlin in the ribs and Ike turned. Tiny came up the steps, carrying the huge Allison easily enough, despite Bob's size. He had the cowboy slung over one great shoulder, an arm steadying the limp form.

"Where'll I put him, Boss?" Tiny asked.

"Throw him down on the floor."

Tiny literally obeyed, and Allison rolled over. His head lolled on his shoulders. Hatfield, always sure that Devlin was close, went over and looked down. Allison was totally out. He hardly recognized the handsome young fellow, for the waddy's face was swollen, with dried blood and scabs on it. There was a dark area in his hair, where he had been struck on the head. His eyes were shut and black patches were under them. Cords bound his feet and ankles, and it was plain he had been viciously beaten and abused.

"Give me that pitcher of water," ordered Varron.

He dashed the water into Allison's face. They watched, and after a few minutes, Allison's eyelids fluttered. He looked up, still dazed, biting at his bloody lip.

"Curse yuh!" he gasped. "Yuh'll pay for this! Yuh'll —" He recognized Hatfield as the supposed friend who had been riding with Doris Lee, and a fresh blaze of anger came into his eyes. "Why, yuh dirty, lyin' —"

"Shut up!" snarled the Ranger, kicking him. He pulled his foot at the last moment although his booted toe dug Allison's ribs and knocked what little wind was left from the cowboy's strained lungs. "Come on, Ike, let's pick him up. We'll tie the skunk on a hoss. We better get started, for we have to ride the long way around. Canty said not to take him across Square L range."

"Here, I'll give yuh a hand," offered the tremendous Tiny.

Varron watched, frowning. He followed them to the porch, and Allison was slung over a saddle, secured with ropes, while

119

Hatfield kept Devlin always by him, never giving him a chance to wink. The uncomfortable Devlin took the lead-rope of Allison's animal and started off ahead, while Hatfield, with a careless wave to Duke Varron, brought up the rear.

"See yuh again soon, Duke," he sang out.

As rapidly as he dared, Hatfield pushed the pace, out of Varron's stronghold, past the sentry boxes on the trail. Devlin was his pass, and they made half a mile and hit the road.

Hatfield glanced back then. A large cloud of dust was coming and on the clear stretch not far behind, he saw Duke Varron and a score of his fighters galloping after him. He swore, inwardly. They were too close to outride, and had sighted the trio.

"Now what?" he thought.

Devlin slowly looked around, licking his lips.

"It — it ain't my fault, Jim," he faltered. "Yuh seen I never give Duke no warnin' —"

"Dry up. I'll handle it."

Varron rapidly overtook them, and fell in by Hatfield.

"Thought I'd go in and talk to Canty myself, Barry. We'll ride to town with yuh." He called to a couple of his men. "Scout the way, boys."

Two horsemen galloped out in front, and the whole party moved down the trail.

Hatfield never turned a hair. Devlin was afraid, afraid something would go sour, that the big man would blame him for it. They made two miles, and then the outriders came plunging back.

"Here comes the Square L, Duke!" the leading man reported.

Varron instantly took charge. "Get up into that draw, pronto!" he ordered. "They didn't see yuh, did they, Ken?"

"No," replied the scout. "They're crossin' the flat. We sighted their dust first."

"They can't see ours, with that crest and the chaparral in the way," remarked Varron. "We'll let 'em get into the cut and then pepper 'em. Hide yore hosses in there — pronto now."

In the crush, Hatfield had a hard time staying close to Devlin. The gunnies concealed themselves rapidly, and waited, a death-trap for the party of cowmen rapidly headed toward the Lazy C.

Big Ed Lee, the Nortons, the Pruets, a couple of dozen stalwart Texans were in the bunch. They were searching for Bob Allison, and had trailed his horse in this direction. Squatted low behind rocks and thorny bush, Duke Varron would catch them in the narrowing cut through the ridges, and slaughter them.

Hatfield sighted them through the chaparral, riding in close formation. Duke Varron had unshipped his shotgun and his own and other murderous muzzles rose to shatter Lee and his friends. The Square L men were on Lazy C range and, with the war on, Varron needed no further excuse. He could plead self-defense, say the Square L had come to attack.

"Can't let 'em ride into this," thought Hatfield.

Devlin had dismounted. He held the lead-rope of the rangy brown mustang across which the gagged and trussed Allison lay. He was watching Hatfield, watching for some chance to betray him without the surety of death that reposed in the tall man's guns.

Closer and closer rode the Square L, as the killers waiting for them cocked their weapons.

CHAPTER XIII:
FIGHT IN THE DRAW

Quick eyes showed Jim Hatfield that he had picked a spot where the rock bluff had crumbled, and that chunks of red stone had rolled down to form a jagged, semicircular pile close to the wall.

"It'll have to do," he thought grimly, girding himself.

He drew in a deep breath, ready for a desperate stand.

Devlin's eyes glowed as he pinned them to the tall man he feared. If Hatfield turned his back, even for an instant —

The Ranger moved with deliberate speed. The coordination of his strong muscles were not disturbed by the dangers of the situation, though, surrounded as he was by quick-trigger experts who would gladly drill him at a word from Duke Varron, death was very close. He seized the moment when Varron and the majority of his gunnies were picking hidden positions from which to shoot the Square L men.

Whipping out his knife, he calmly cut the bonds holding Allison, who was in a semi-comatose condition from the long hours of abuse to which he had been subjected. Devlin's eyes widened but he dared not say anything, as Hatfield pulled the heavy Allison off the far side of the Lazy C mustang to which he had been tied, and stepped toward the rock nest a few yards up the draw.

"Come on, Ike," he said in a low, commanding voice, and Devlin slowly walked with him.

"S-s-st!"

Duke Varron was hissing at them. He had looked around and seen Hatfield and Devlin headed for the upper section of the split.

But the Ranger was close to the protective bulwark. He pushed Allison sideward, so that Square L puncher fell to the ground, shielded by stone. With a quick leap, he seized Ike Devlin's wrist and jumped behind the rocks.

Raising his six-shooter, the Ranger fired two blasts of triple shots, due warning of danger that the Square L could not ignore. He heard shouts from Lee's party.

"Yuh fool!" Varron screamed. "Yuh've warned 'em! They're splittin'! Fire, dang yuh, fire!"

Blasting guns roared from the hidden draw, rattling their horrid threats in the calm day.

But the trap-trigger had been pulled too soon by Hatfield for the killers' fire to do much damage. The range was long, and only a couple of Lee's friends felt the touch of lead, as they hastily split, riding out to the sides and drawing their weapons. Bullets began blasting back at Varron and his men.

Duke, his face flaming scarlet, turned, his Colts rising toward the nest of rocks. Suspicion blazed in his eyes as he saw the Ranger down behind the stones, and Allison gone. Varron started swiftly that way, signaling half a dozen men with him.

Hatfield, a fresh pistol in hand, had to stop them. The Square L, shocked by the unexpected gunfire from the draw, had turned back. They were riding off, split up, and shooting wild ones in the foe's direction. They had been saved from the death-trap, thanks to the Ranger, and Duke Varron was coming for revenge against Hatfield.

Ike Devlin squatted beside Hatfield, but the Ranger had to concentrate on the foes massing at the lower end of the draw, and could only glimpse Devlin from the corner of his eye. He had to watch Varron.

"Stand back, Duke!" Hatfield sang out.

Varron stopped, hesitated. Hatfield saw him call more men about him, and then the hard-eyed gunnies all swung to finish him. Varron was sure now that Hatfield was an enemy. All his suspicions were verified by the Ranger's actions.

"I'll have to wing Duke to check 'em," decided the Ranger, and took aim at Varron.

But Devlin now saw his chance. With a desperate curse, he whipped a hidden six-gun from inside his shirt and threw it against the Ranger's side. Hatfield caught the man's flicking move, sensed what might happen. His Colt bellowed but it was already slashing down to strike against Devlin's forearm, deflect his pistol. His shot missed Duke, but he connected with Ike, and Devlin's hot muzzle was turned enough to save the Ranger from instant death.

However, the heavy bullet from Devlin's Colt cut a deep gash in the flesh and muscles under Hatfield's shoulder. It stung with agonizing, deep-seated pain, caught at his breath. He fought off the sickening sensations and seized Ike as Devlin screamed:

"Help! He's a spy! Workin' for Lee!"

Hatfield had him now, was ripping away Devlin's revolver, and in his mighty fury lifting him clear of the ground. He held the squirming, scratching, screeching Devlin, long fingers digging into the man's body. Whirling Devlin around, he straightened up and hurled the man through the air, across the top of the jagged rocks.

Kicking and clawing air, Devlin was hurled into space. But Varron had heard what he shouted, and Duke and his men had let go their lead a breath before. A dozen .45 slugs rapped into Devlin and he was dead before he bounced on the ground outside the nest.

Hatfield began firing hotly, bobbing up. His bullets breathed too close for comfort, and Varron, protected by a ring of his men, realized he would lose heavily if he kept charging.

"Take cover, boys!" he roared, above the bang of the guns.

Slugs searched for the Ranger. His side was bleeding like a running faucet, and he was panting from the terrible exertion.

The Ranger's Colts belched the threat of death. He wanted to down Duke Varron, the leader of the gunmen, and smash the resistance. Coming up in different spots, Hatfield tried for Varron. The shotguns, spraying out, shrieked their loads like hail, spattering the rocks, whistling in the air over Hatfield's bulwark.

He threw down a hot revolver, drew his last loaded weapon. When he had emptied it, he was forced to reload, and Varron guessed what the few instants of lull meant.

"Charge, boys!" he shrieked. "His guns are out!"

Hatfield, with four slugs in the revolver chambers, snapped it shut and hurriedly threw a couple at them. They split, hunting protection from his fire.

Something touched the Ranger's skull then, something that burned with irresistible power. Lights danced before his gray-green eyes, blinding lights, and the killers out there wavered before him. Colt in hand, Hatfield slowly sank in front of the weakened, half-senseless Allison . . .

When Hatfield came back to himself, he was lying on a clean cot in an airy room. Morning sunlight streamed in at the open window, and Doris Lee sat beside his bed, watching him with troubled eyes.

"Well?" he murmured, looking up at her.

She smiled and sighed with relief.

"Oh, I'm so glad! How do you feel?"

"Sorta washed-out," he told her. "But I'm hungry."

He felt weak and it was good to lie there.

His shoulder was heavily padded by a bandage, fastened around his chest, and the hair had been cut away from the scalp wound and a dressing stuck on.

"I'll bring you some broth," Doris said eagerly. "The doctor said you could have some when you came to."

"Doctor? He got here mighty fast. And it's powerful early. I thought it was later."

"Why, it's Friday! It was yesterday morning that you were in that fight with the Lazy C."

"That so? I've been out a long while."

"You woke up for a while, but you were delirious. Father and the boys got up on the banks of the draw and drove Duke Varron and his men off just in time to save Bob and you."

"Allison's all right?"

"Yes, he'll be fine. He has to rest for a few days, that's all. He wasn't seriously injured — this time."

Bob Allison appeared in the door, hearing their voices. His face was bruised and still swollen, and he limped heavily. He came in and touched Hatfield's hand.

"Yuh'll have to forgive me, Jim," he growled. "I didn't savvy yuh were on our side. When I saw yuh walkin' around loose at Varron's, I figgered yuh was one of 'em, specially since yuh'd saved Devlin from us. And I was sort of groggy up there in the draw, durin' the fight. But Lee and the others say yuh protected me with yore body. We were in that rock nest where yuh fought the Lazy C off."

"It's true I'm with yuh, Allison," Hatfield told him, then asked, "Duke got away?"

Allison nodded. "Yeah. He was nicked, and so were several of his men. One was killed — Ike Devlin. Lee's goin' to complain to the sheriff when he's in town."

"I'd like to speak to him," Hatfield declared. "Got some things to plan."

"Dad isn't here," Doris informed him. "When he got in with Bob and you yesterday, there was a message waiting for him from Pecosville. He left last evening and hasn't come back yet."

"That so? What was the message?"

"He didn't say," replied the girl. "But I'll go now and fix you something to eat."

After a light meal, Hatfield felt well enough to smoke, propped up in his cot. The doctor, brought out from Pecosville, had advised that he lie up for several days, but the Ranger was aware of the dangers delay meant. Canty and Varron, defeated by him in their attempt to kill Bob Allison, would move quickly. Of that he was certain.

He heard sounds out in the yard, and the calling voices of Square L cowboys. Then, glancing through, he saw Doris hurrying to the front door, followed by her mother.

After a time, he caught the sobbing of the women, and soon Bob Allison came limping up to the Ranger's door, and looked in. His face was a mask of anguish.

"They just brought Ed Lee's corpse back from town, Jim," he reported somberly.

Hatfield started, violently. Pain went through his stiffened, wounded side.

"Shot?" he growled.

Allison shook his head. "No. He died of heart failure. Natural enough, I reckon, seein' how much he's been stirred up lately. But it's an awful blow just the same."

"That's tough," muttered the Ranger. "Time I was up and goin'."

Bob Allison went back to Doris and her mother, the stricken women whose loved one had died. Cowboys, hats off, faces woebegone, carried the body inside the house. As they laid the remains of Big Ed Lee, a fair and square man, on the living-room couch, Jim Hatfield, boots and guns on, appeared from the side room where he had lain.

"Yuh better go back and lie down, Jim," Allison told him.

The Ranger was drawn but he had reserves of strength; clean living, terrific power, kept him going. The first shock of the wounds had worn off and he could act.

Swiftly he viewed Big Ed Lee. There was not a mark of violence on the giant rancher, although there was a strained look to his pallid face and his throat cords were drawn in rigor mortis. Hatfield stared at the body, the sobbing of the women in his ears.

He swung on a Square L cowboy, one who had brought the corpse back from Pecosville on a flat wagon.

"Yuh rode to town with yore boss?" he asked.

"Yeah," replied the waddy. "We got in round ten last night. The boss took eight of us along."

"Nobody laid hands on him?"

"Not that we saw. Anyways, he ain't marked."

"Huh." Hatfield thought it over. "Come outside, Buck, I'd like to talk to yuh."

On the porch, he interrogated the waddy, "Buck."

"Miss Doris says yore boss got a message from town, and that sent him in. Is that right?"

Buck shrugged his shoulders.

"Reckon so. He just called us and told us

to saddle up and come along. When we got to town, we went over to a vacant house near Mayor Barry's place. Lee ordered us to string a circle around it and we did. Then he went in, gun drawn and ready for trouble. We didn't hear nothin' and the place stayed dark. Nobody went in or out. We waited till we was wore out, and then we decided we'd go in and see what was up. The boss was sitting slumped in a chair behind the closed door, in the front room. Nobody with him, and no signs of a fight. The sawbones said his heart had quit."

It was a puzzle. Hatfield rolled a quirly, handed Buck the makin's, and lit up.

"Who brought the message that took Lee to town?" he asked them.

"I was out with the boss, at the draw fight. But Miss Doris told her dad that a young feller who works around the saloons fetched it out. Said somebody he didn't know had give him five dollars to deliver it."

"It was a written message?"

"Yeah, I reckon so."

Hatfield couldn't find the letter. Doris said it had been sealed, addressed to her father in pencil printing.

"Queer doin's," the Ranger thought. "Now where's that note?"

Despite the physician's verdict concerning

Lee's death, Hatfield was suspicious. The coincidence was too marked for him to let this slide. He began turning over possibilities as to the fate of the letter which had sent Ed Lee to Pecosville in such a rush.

"It's a break for Canty — just what he's prayed for," he mused.

After a time, he went back into the main room, and to the open fireplace. Burnt sticks, and the charred remains of papers were on the stone hearth. He found the corner of an envelope.

"Must have burnt it," he concluded.

Squatted down, he stuck his head and shoulders in. There was a damper bar at the mouth of the chimney, narrowing down to create its draft. Something white was stuck there, and he reached in, picked out a partially consumed sheet of white paper.

There was printing in pencil on it, and he was able to read some of the words. The note had been set afire by a match, and tossed into the fireplace. The draft had blown it up, and the flame had gone out, leaving it stuck on the damper bar. He made out:

. . . evidence against Canty, but come *alone. Burn this.*

That was all he could read. He was certain, however, that this was the communication which had sent Lee hurrying to Pecosville, there to die of — the doctor said heart-failure.

"That printin' looks mighty like what I saw on the order Canty sent Duke Varron," he decided.

He slipped out to the stables. Goldy had been led in by Lee's men and was rested, unharmed, waiting for him in the corral. The sorrel came to him on call, and he cinched up, mounted and hit the trail to town.

Chapter XIV:
Marked for Death

Dark had fallen when the Ranger reached Pecosville where lamplight sparkled in the clean, tangy air. He swung around the plaza toward Mayor Barry's home and as he turned in, he was challenged by alert sentries, men armed with double-barreled shotguns patrolling the place.

"Who's that?" called Barry. He was in the kitchen, from where the appetizing odors of Mercedes' cooking floated out.

"It's Jim, Uncle Jake!" Hatfield called back.

"Let him through, boys."

Mercedes had a broad smile on her face as Hatfield limped into the kitchen. He sat down, rather quickly, feeling the effects of his injuries and the swift ride. The Mexican woman cried out and hurried to his side, stroking his cheek.

"Poor boy, he ees hurt! *Si,* look, Senor Barry, he ees hurt!"

"What in thunder hit yuh, Jim?" inquired Barry. "I heard somethin' about a fight on the range and that yuh was in it."

Hatfield explained briefly. Then he said:

"Lee's dead. Yuh reckon Canty's responsible?"

Mayor Barry shook his white head. "Nope, absolutely not, Jim. It so happens that Canty was in the Prairie Fire Saloon, all that evenin'. Saw him myself, and I didn't leave there till close to eleven o'clock. They say Canty never stirred from his table till midnight."

"He's got it mighty pat," thought the Ranger. "Canty's shore covered."

Hatfield needed rest, more strength. He ate the supper Mercedes lovingly pressed upon him, but before he turned in for a real sleep he saw through his window that the well-digger's house was quiet.

In the morning, he accompanied Jake Barry to the vacant house where Big Ed Lee had been found dead.

"This is one of my properties," explained Barry. "Not rented at present. Lee was sittin' on that old chair in this room when they found him. Heart quit, I guess. Too much fightin' and excitement for a man his age."

Hatfield felt a great deal better after his full sleep, and his head was clearer for work.

He ranged about the room, but found nothing that provided him with a clue. A few odds-and-ends of furniture, including the backless chair, had been left by the previous tenants. There was a single window, nailed shut, and narrow door, at the bottom of which a strip of oilcloth had been tacked to cut off the drafts.

The Ranger's high heel hit a loose board, and he nearly fell, but with his catlike agility, he recovered his balance.

"This is too good to be true, for Canty," he thought, keeping his hunch to himself.

"Where yuh goin' now, Jim?" asked Barry.

"Outside."

Hatfield went to the side of the house, squatted down and looked underneath it. The soil was loose and sandy. The building was set on logs driven into the ground, and he could crawl under on his hands and knees. The dirt had been freshly disturbed, of that he was sure. He found a stick and scratched around, but there was nothing.

Voices sent him creeping forth. George Canty was standing close by, talking to Barry.

"Why, hello, Jim," Canty said, smiling. "What yuh doin' under there? Diggin'? Need any help?"

"I reckon," drawled Hatfield, feeling the

same cold shivers in Canty's presence he had felt before; that instinctive menace and dislike. "Yuh're expert at that, Canty, I hear."

"Yuh mean diggin'?" said Canty, blinking. "Yeah, yuh're right, boy. If yuh have a mind for that sort of work, just let me know and I'll take yuh on."

The sunlight glinted on the man's coarse red hair. He wore his black hat, cocked jauntily on one side of the red head, a new shirt with fancy pearl buttons, and a red silk bandanna. He had recently shaved, too, and his freckled features had been scrubbed. Canty was all spruced up, but his cat eyes never left Hatfield's taut face.

"He'll kill me the instant he thinks there's a chance," Hatfield thought. "I've got to beat him to it . . ."

Back on the Square L spread, where Jim Hatfield had left men and women mourning for Big Ed Lee, Bob Allison knew that he must act as a tower of strength, to help Doris Lee and her mother through the terrible days of their bereavement. Mrs. Lee, stricken by the death of her husband, had finally collapsed and Doris had insisted her mother take to her bed.

The funeral for which Hatfield had not waited, as an outsider, had been simple, and had taken place that morning, the day after Lee had been brought home. Nearby, on a windswept hill was the cairn of stones and the wooden cross marking big Ed Lee's grave for he had expressed the desire to be buried on his own range. In the late afternoon, Mrs. Lee, who had not slept at all since they brought Lee home, had finally fallen into the sleep of sheer exhaustion.

Doris came out, and Allison at once joined her. For these young folks, life was just beginning, and they had the resiliency of youth and the powers of quick recuperation from shock. They were deeply in love, and the girl leaned on Allison's arm as they strolled together out in the yard.

"How's yore mother?" he asked.

He felt clumsy, helpless, much as he wished to be of assistance. Doris seemed to take great comfort just from his presence, however.

"She's sleeping," replied Doris, in a low, steady voice.

Outwardly, she seemed entirely calm, but as Allison held her hand tightly, he could feel that her whole body was tense.

"Bob" she said, "the Square L belongs to Mother and me now. I want to sell it at once and get out. We can start fresh somewhere else."

Allison started. "Why, Doris! Yuh'd have to take a low price, and lose thousands, sellin' in such a hurry. Besides, I can run the ranch for yore mother and you and make it pay. That's what I've been thinkin'. You know yuh can trust me. It's not like havin' a foreman who is not interested in yuh."

"I want to go away from here."

"But — why? 'Cause yore dad's dead? Folks don't pack up and leave their homes when a loved one passes on."

"It isn't because Father's gone. That is, not if he died a natural death."

"But he did. The doc says so. Wasn't a mark on him."

She shook her head. Intuition was all she had to base her decisions on.

"I — I'm afraid," she whispered, clinging to him, shivering.

"Of Canty?"

Doris nodded. Allison knew that she was not a coward. She was as brave as any pioneer woman and the blood in her veins made her a fighter.

"It — it's the way I feel," she tried to explain. "First my brother, and now Dad. You've had several narrow escapes. They'll kill you sooner or later. It's Canty — I know it!"

"Yeah, Canty shot Jack. But he never touched yore father. And he can't get at us here because we have too many men for him. The law's on our side, ain't it?"

"We have no legal proof that will send Canty to prison, where he ought to be. He got away with killing Jack, and now there isn't a shred of evidence against him as to Father. I — I know he'll try for you again, Bob. And I love you too much to lose you. I couldn't stand it if — if —"

She was crying, softly, and Allison was terribly perturbed.

"I can't stand to see yuh cry, Doris," he begged. "Shucks! Quit worryin', now. I'll take care of everything."

In his youthful power, Bob Allison was sure of himself, sure that he could run the Square L and attend to everything.

"Yuh, savvy, dear," he argued, "that yore property controls all this range. If yuh sold it to some stranger, for a song, why all our friends would be at the new owner's mercy as to water."

"That's so," agreed Doris.

At last she said he was right, that they could not leave their home, and Allison was greatly relieved.

"I'll saddle a couple of broncs and we'll have a little ride, Doris," he urged. "It'll make yuh feel better to exercise."

"All right. I'll go in and get ready."

Allison slapped hulls on two horses. He loved to dash over the rolling land with the girl he loved, with the aromatic breeze of the Trans-Pecos in his face. Soon Doris appeared in her riding clothes, and they mounted. She was an expert rider, and had been born to the saddle.

They went farther than they expected to, absorbed in one another, and in the freedom of the beautiful range. As the spirited mustangs slowed, after a swift gallop, several men pushed from a heavy mesquite clump close to the trail they were on.

"George Canty!" Bob Allison roared as he jerked his horse to a sliding stop, his right hand dropping to his Colt.

The red-haired well-digger was surrounded by half a dozen of his workmen, heavy-browed, powerful fellows. Among them were Morg, Lefty, and Tim, and all were armed.

"Hold yore gun, Allison!" cried Canty, raising his hand in a gesture of peace. "I've come to speak to Miss Doris!"

The girl saw at once that, if a fight began, Allison would be overwhelmed, shot down. She touched the mustang's ribs with a spur rowel, and the animal jumped, placing her between Allison and Canty's party.

"Stop — don't draw your gun, Bob!" she ordered shrilly.

"I don't mean no harm," Canty called. "All I want is a word with yuh, Miss Doris."

"Yuh can't talk to her — yuh ain't fit!" bawled the enraged Allison, hand still on his Colt butt. "Get offa the Square L range, Canty, yuh —"

"Put up yore paws," a gruff voice commanded, just behind Allison.

Two more of Canty's men, having crept around the spot where Allison and Doris sat their horses, rose up in back of the Square L foreman, covering him with shotguns.

"We ain't goin' to hurt yuh," Canty said. "I told yuh all I'm after is to talk to Miss Doris. Yuh're keepin' up this here war, not me, Allison. I'd rather be friends."

"Please, Bob, please!" begged Doris, pale and frightened. "For my sake, keep still and do as they say."

She was in terrible fear lest Allison fight against these impossible odds, and die before her eyes. She and Bob had made a mistake, she knew, in riding out so far without a bodyguard of cowboys near at hand.

"I'll go and speak with Canty," she said

quickly. "You wait here."

"No!" snarled Allison, bursting with fury.

But Doris already was walking her horse, toward George Canty. The well-digger sat his black animal solidly, his mighty shoulders hunched, freckled face set. His eyes glinted as the beautiful girl slowly approached him, her gaze pinned to his.

Allison, trembling with rage, started forward. The shotguns leveled on him.

"Bob — Bob! Stop!" Doris screamed.

She was in line of fire. Allison paused, grinding his teeth.

CHAPTER XV:
STARTLING PROPOSAL

Canty pushed out to meet Doris. With his black facing one way, as the girl's horse faced the other, he was close enough to speak in a low voice that only she could hear.

Had Allison been able to catch what Canty said, he would have been so infuriated that nothing could have restrained him, not even the certainty of death at the hands of Canty's men.

"Miss Doris," Canty murmured, "I had to see yuh, speak to yuh and tell yuh how sorry I am yore father died. I want to help yuh and if there's anything I can do, please call on me, any time."

"Thank you," she said, her voice strained. She tried, for Allison's sake, to keep the icy loathing from her tone.

Canty went on, rapidly, speaking his piece:

"Yuh came to see me in town. I promised to do all I could to help yuh, and I meant it. Yuh savvy I had nothin' to do with yore father's death. I come to tell yuh this, that I always wanted to be friends with him because of you. I shore admire yuh. Yuh're the prettiest girl who ever lived."

Doris was horrified, scarcely able to believe her ears. Canty was making love to her, at this moment! She stared, her red lips parted, speechless. His cat eyes never left her face. The egotistical soul of the strange well-digger was bared to her for an instant and fear streaked in her heart.

"I'd do anything to have a chance with yuh, Miss Doris!" he whispered hoarsely. "Will yuh meet me again in town, where we can have a real talk together?"

"No!" she gasped. "Please — you misunderstood! I couldn't ever care about you or even be your friend. I'm going to marry Bob Allison —" She bit her tongue, sorry she had mentioned Bob.

Canty's eyes shadowed over, as though curtains had been drawn down.

"Sorry," he said gruffly. For a moment he stared at the blue sky of the Trans-Pecos, then he said, "I want yuh to savvy I'm still ready to help yuh, and be yore friend. I mean no harm to anyone. We ain't goin' to hurt Allison or you, of course."

Allison, unable to hear what was being

said, waited in tense anger. Doris nodded, and wheeled her horse, as Canty sang out:

"Come on, boys, we're ridin'!"

The well-digger, screened by his powerful gang, turned and headed swiftly along the road to Pecosville.

Allison was left to join Doris. He was sputtering with rage. "What'd he say?" he demanded of Doris.

"He — he only told me he wished to help me," Doris stammered.

She was trembling, and when Allison took her hand he found it clammy and cold.

"Curse his heart and soul, he's give yuh the creeps!" he snarled. "I'll down that crab devil one of these days!"

Doris shook her head, forcing back the tears that threatened. Staring straight ahead, the pleasure of their ride spoiled by the encounter with George Canty, Allison and Doris hurried home.

There was plenty of work to be done at the Square L, and Allison, taking over command, found his hands full. He had fifteen waddies to direct, and stock to see to. He was up at daybreak the following day, and out in the corral yard checking some mustangs that were to be sold soon.

One of his men sang out to him, and Allison looked around, to see the cowboy escorting a thin Mexican boy, riding an oversized gray horse.

"Kid's got a message for yuh, Bob," reported the waddy.

Allison smiled on the boy, and took the letter which the dark-faced youth held out.

"See he gets some breakfast, Ace," he ordered. "And here's four bits for yuh, *muchacho.*"

"Mille gracias, senor."

This was a different lad from the one who had brought a message for Big Ed Lee. Allison opened the envelope, extracted the folded sheet of plain paper. On it was printed, crudely:

Allison. I know plenty on G. Canty. But scared to talk. It will have to be secrit, savvy? If you want to finnesh Canty, meet me secrit in Room 6 of the Buffalo Haid at 9 tomorrer nite. If anywun is with you, you won't even see me. Burn this *now.*

There was no signature, and Allison's chin dropped as he stared at the strange message.

"Now, what in thunder!" he muttered. "Must be somebody knows a lot on Canty and wants to get even!"

149

His mouth watered at the thought of pinning George Canty down and putting him where he belonged, either in a hangman's noose or in prison.

Allison thrust the note into his pocket. He could touch a match to it later. It had all the earmarks of being written by a man who was frightened of his own life, although desiring to get rid of George Canty. He strode around to the bunkhouse shack, and the cook was feeding the Mexican youth.

"Say Bub, who give yuh that letter to me?" he demanded, seizing the scrawny wrist.

"Senor, an hombre I no savvy," replied the lad in his broken English. "He say, tak' eet to Senor All-ee-son at Square L. He geev me too dollaires."

A stranger to the boy had paid him to bring the note out.

Allison went outside, walking up and down, thinking it out. Looming in his mind was the thought of the relief they would all feel, with George Canty convicted and put out of the way by the law. It would settle the war, and all their worries.

"I'll go!" he decided. "I'll have some of the boys foller me at a distance, though, so's I won't be in danger."

Obeying the written word of the communication he had received, Allison read it carefully again, and then touched a match to it, stamping the charred remains into the sandy dirt of the yard.

"Jim," reported Mayor Jake Barry. "Sheriff Frank Miles just pulled into town. He's over at the marshal's office. Yuh want to talk to him, don't yuh?"

"Yeah," replied Hatfield. "Can yuh fetch him over here, Mr. Barry?"

They were in Barry's parlor. Hatfield, recuperating from his injuries, had checked up on Canty as far as he could in Pecosville. McDowell had okayed Sheriff Miles, and the county officer would make a strong ally.

"Shore, I'll go get him," agreed the mayor.

Hatfield waited. He wished his conference with the sheriff to be in secret. After a time, Barry appeared, walking with a square-bodied, bullet-headed man who wore a long brown mustache on his sun-red face. He was bow-legged from living on horseback, and rolled from side to side as he moved. A dark Stetson, a leather jacket and chaps made up Miles' costume.

Barry led him inside, and Miles glanced up into the gray-green depths of the Ranger's long-lashed eyes.

"Well, well, so this is yore nephew!"

exclaimed Miles, startled at the size of the mighty Ranger. "He sorta makes up for you, Jake!"

Miles guffawed at his own trite jest. He broke off suddenly, however, jaw dropping, as he saw the silver star on the silver circle, emblem of the Texas Rangers, which Hatfield exposed in his cupped hand.

"Cuss my hide!" he cried. "So you boys are in! I'm glad to see yuh."

"Keep it quiet," ordered Hatfield. "McDowell says yuh're a good man to work with, Miles. He okayed yuh."

"He did, huh? That's mighty fine." The sheriff's chest expanded and his eyes flashed. When the Rangers recommended a man, it meant something. "What can I do for yuh?"

"I come over to stop this war. You arrested Canty, when young Lee was killed, didn't yuh?"

"Yeah, or rather, he heard we was huntin' him and surrendered to me. He had an iron-clad alibi, give him by Duke Varron and several of his men. Jury couldn't hang him on such evidence. I figger Allison was off his conk from bein' wounded and thought he spied Canty."

"Mebbe, mebbe," drawled the Ranger. "Though from what I've learned, Sheriff,

Canty ain't beyond dry-gulchin' an enemy. Now look here. Yuh better get out to the Lazy C, Duke Varron's spread, and arrest the whole passel of gunnies yuh find there."

"On what charges?" inquired Miles.

"Kidnapin', for one thing. They held Bob Allison a prisoner there, and nearly beat his face off. Hoss stealin', if yuh want another reason. They still have Allison's hoss, or they had it. And gunnin' me and the Square L men. There's no lack of charges. Big thing is to hold 'em in the calaboose till I can catch up with Canty. I've no real evidence yet agin Canty, but I'll have it pronto. Canty's responsible for all the ructions raised in these parts, and he's goin' to pay. Duke Varron's his man and does as Canty orders. I'm hopin' to scare somethin' out of Varron when we collar him."

Hatfield paused, letting this sink in.

Miles scratched his sandy-haired bullethead. "My boys are wore out, Ranger. We rode eighty miles in the last day. They'll need a little rest 'fore we start."

There was, thought the Ranger, always this human element to be considered in a campaign. Men could only do so much.

"How many yuh got with yah, Miles?" he inquired.

"Twelve. I can swear in more here,

though."

Hatfield shook his head. "No, I don't want to scare Canty. It'd tip him off. He'd guess what went on. I don't believe the Lazy C'll fight yuh, Sheriff. They think their noses are clean and they won't want to go outlaw if it can be helped. But we don't want to warn 'em. Yore men will be ready by dawn tomorrer, won't they?"

"Yeah, that'll be fine."

"Rout 'em out early, then, feed 'em, and make shore they're well-heeled. But don't ride toward the Lazy C. Instead, head south as though yuh were goin' back where yuh come from. Circle when yuh're well out of sight, and ride cross country. I'll meet yuh at the forks leadin' to Varron's."

"Right. I'm yore man, Ranger."

The Sheriff saluted Hatfield, and rolled out. Barry said, face troubled: "That Canty's an eel. He got away with murder, I reckon, and he expects to agin."

"Yuh're right there, Mr. Barry." The Ranger nodded grimly. "We've got to check him, and pronto!"

Hatfield's back was still a bit stiff, and a scab had formed on the shallow crease in his scalp. However, he felt a good deal stronger and knew that a full night's sleep would restore his full power. After Merce-

des had plied him with a delicious supper,
he turned in.

CHAPTER XVI:
TURN-OFF

Before the new day broke Jim Hatfield was up, ready for work. Mercedes heard him in the kitchen. She slept in a lean-to at the rear of the house, and soon came bustling in, with her wide grin, and fixed him a hot breakfast that hit the right spot.

"Yuh've shore been a big help Mercedes," the Ranger told her. "A man could fight wildcats on feeds like you hand out."

"Nize boy — be careful," she warned, patting him.

"That's not so easy in my business, Mercedes," replied the Ranger dryly.

Out at the stable, he found Goldy well-rested and eager to go. The sorrel nuzzled him lovingly as Hatfield slapped his hull on the gelding, cinched up, checked his weapons and gear, and swung into the leather seat.

Nothing moved on Canty's side of town. Hatfield picked the back alleys, avoiding the well-digger's, and was soon in the chaparral fringing the muddy creek, north of Pecosville, and headed for the Lazy C, Varron's outfit. The shortest route ran across Square L range, and the crossroads where he was to meet Sheriff Miles was a stiff run ahead.

The sun was high when the Ranger, whose keen eyes seldom missed anything of importance, sighted a rider coming from the north trail that skirted the creek. This was the side road to Lee's Square L. However, the horseman, whoever he was, did not keep to the beaten track but rode in open country, skirting clumps of mesquite, and other chaparral and the high rocks that cropped up here and there.

Hatfield paused, observing him for a time, from behind the crest of a ridge where he sat his sorrel. The man was a long way off at first, but he was approaching the Ranger's position as he moved.

"He's mighty wary," thought Hatfield, as he saw how the fellow zigzagged and slowed to check dangerous spots.

As he drew nearer, the Ranger decided that he knew who it might be. The way he sat his horse and his figure were familiar. Soon Hatfield was able to recognize Bob Allison, the light-haired young foreman of the Square L.

"Now what's he think he's doin', ridin' alone toward Pecosville!" he muttered. "He's takin' a big chance!"

He dropped Goldy back, and cantered along the ridge, keeping out of Allison's vision until he was within five hundred yards of the rider. Allison, low over a big gray mustang, rode at full-tilt past Hatfield's hiding place, and the Ranger hailed him.

Allison swung his gray around with a violent jerk of the reins, startled at the call. Then he recognized Hatfield, as the Ranger pushed the sorrel over.

"Howdy, Allison," drawled Hatfield. "Where yuh bound?"

Allison blinked, did not reply at once. Then he said: "Why, to town, Jim."

"Ridin' this range alone is mighty dangerous, specially after what's happened to yuh, Allison. Must be mighty important to take yuh to Pecosville at this time and this way."

"Yeah, it is." Allison seemed ill at ease, and trying to hide it.

"Yuh are by yoreself, then?"

"Well — I'll tell yuh. Some of my men are comin' in, but by a different route."

"I see." Hatfield added, "Miles and I are goin' after Varron."

"I got to get somethin' needed a lot at the ranch, or I'd shore like to go along with

158

yuh," Bob said regretfully.

"Oh." Hatfield thought it over, then he said, "Well, watch yoreself. Remember, Canty and Varron are not foolin'."

"Thanks, Jim."

Allison was in a sweat to get along and the Ranger let him go. Hatfield rode for a time, but then pulled up, and turned. He could see Allison's dust headed toward town.

"I can't let him go in there, not with Canty on the prowl," he mused. "I'll have to stop him and find out what he's hidin' from me."

His suspicion had grown greater and greater. It was only too obvious that his waddy friend was concealing something from him.

Shortcutting, with Allison zigzagging and checking possible ambushes, the Ranger caught up with the Square L man a couple of miles south of where he had first met him. His hail again startled the foreman.

"I thought yuh was on yore way to the Lazy C," Allison said, surprised, as Hatfield drew up beside him.

"I was. I'm s'posed to meet Sheriff Miles at the crossroads . . . Allison, let's talk turkey. I'm a Texas Ranger, and here to settle this trouble."

"A Ranger! Say, I never guessed it, Jim."

"My right name is Hatfield, Jim Hatfield. I told Big Ed Lee who I was, just as I did Mayor Barry. I'm not the mayor's nephew, but we cooked up that story to fool anybody who might be inclined to wonder what was I doin' in Pecosville."

Hatfield paused, staring at Allison. When the foreman did not speak, the Ranger said:

"Well?"

"Well, what?"

"I've been frank and open with you, Bob," drawled Hatfield. "S'pose you be the same with me."

Allison looked confused; then he swore, and said:

"All right, Jim. I didn't say anything, for I was afraid yuh'd try to stop me, and I'm set on goin' through with something. I got a note from somebody in town who's got a grudge against Canty. This party, who didn't sign his name to the letter, claims he'll give me vital evidence against Canty, and that's what I want. I figger, with Canty out of the picture, we'll all be a lot safer. I'm on my way there now. I was told to come alone, so I had my men go by a different route. They'll connect with me in town after dark, when we won't be spotted."

"I see." The Ranger was glad that he had come back after his youthful friend. "Allison, it's lucky I decided to force yore hand this time. Ed Lee received the same sort of note just before he died. I know more of what's goin' on than you do, naturally enough, since I've been workin' from several sides. Do yuh realize that yuh're prob'ly walkin' into the same sort of trap Lee did?"

Allison blinked. "Trap? How can there be a trap, Jim? Lee died of heart failure, didn't he?"

"Mebbe. Mebbe not." Hatfield's face was a set mask, unreadable, grim. "Where's the note?"

"I burned it, like it said."

"Lee threw his into the fireplace. The draft lifted it up and it caught in a damper handle. Yuh're travelin' the same trail yore boss did, Bob. What'd yore note say?"

"Well, that this here party knew plenty about George Canty but was scared to tell it open-like. He would do so in secret, if I'd meet him at nine tonight in Room Six of the Buffalo Head Saloon in Pecosville. I was to come alone or he wouldn't show up."

"Reckoned it was somethin' like that," murmured the Ranger.

The hunch which had sent him back after Allison had been a sound one. He had his appointment to keep with Sheriff Miles, but he could not allow Allison to walk into a death-trap nor could he afford to miss such a chance as this offered, where he might be able to catch the hidden killer who was after the foreman.

"How soon yuh expect to pick up yore men?" he asked.

"At dark, two miles from town. We're meetin' at an old log bridge across the crik."

"Sheriff'll just have to wait till I can get a message to him," decided Hatfield. This was the main line, for the Ranger had deduced that Varron was a side issue.

They rested for a time, having a snack from their saddle-bags, and a drink. Riding on, they waited on the heights, with the town a collection of dark spots by the creek.

Night had fallen when Allison's men arrived, dusty from a roundabout run through chaparral and hilly country. The Ranger wrote out a message to Miles, and despatched it to the crossroads by one of Allison's Square L waddies. He had Allison write a note to Ollie Norton, asking Norton to gather the ranchers and come to town.

"Yuh'll meet that hombre, whoever he is, on schedule, Bob," instructed the Ranger. "I'm goin' to try to trap *him*. You'll be the bait."

"Suits me." Allison nodded.

"We may run into opposition in Pecosville. Canty's got men around, but with yore pards, we can check it."

When the Square L men were rested — Allison had six riders to act as his guard — they moved carefully toward the town, Hatfield directing the approach. He gave instructions to Allison and to the others.

"We'll make Barry's barn now," he told them, "and get a hot meal and a rest there, till it's time for Bob to meet this feller we're after."

Scouting the way, the Ranger pulled in around eight o'clock in the alleyway behind Barry's place. He could see the house lights; the kitchen door was open. The town seemed to be humming more than usual, and among the sounds drifting to him against the wind, Hatfield distinguished a shrill wailing.

Dismounting in the shadows, Hatfield headed for the kitchen door. The wailing was louder in his ears now, and he realized it was Mercedes, Barry's old Mexican cook and housekeeper.

"Ai-ai, ai-ai!" she shrilled.

Her cries filled the house. He went swiftly up the hall, and there the old woman was, bent over the couch in the parlor and weeping as though her heart had been broken.

Hatfield started as he saw the shape of a man lying on the sofa. Some of Pecosville's citizens were around. He did not wish to show himself, so tip-toed around where he could get a clearer view. The doctor appeared in the doorway, and way was made for him.

The doctor patted Mercedes kindly, saying:

"Yuh better go lie down, Mercedes. There's nothin' more to be done. He's dead."

Hatfield could see the white face of the man on the sofa now. And it was Mayor Jake Barry, his friend!

CHAPTER XVII: THE ENEMY

Shocked to the core, Hatfield strode through into the lighted parlor.

"Mercedes!" he called.

She rose from her knees, and went to him, clutching his arm, the tears streaming down her wrinkled brown cheeks.

"He ees dead, he ees dead!" she moaned.

Hatfield sought to comfort her but she was inconsolable. Caring for the man she served had become her life.

"What happened, Doc?" growled the Ranger, leaving the old woman to neighbors who had come in.

"Shucks, Jim," Dr. Grumman replied, "I got a call from a feller who tends bar at the Last Chance that somethin' was wrong with Mayor Barry. I hustled over, and they'd found Barry lying by a room door in the back of the saloon. He was gone when I arrived, and they fetched him here. Then I come back, as the old Mex woman begged me to. But he's through."

Hatfield had made a quick examination of the body.

"Only mark I see is that bluish-black bruise on the side of the head, Doc. Yuh find anything else?"

"Nope. It was heart failure. After all pore Jake was over seventy and yuh've got to expect it at that age, any time. That bruise is where he hit when he fell."

"Like Ed Lee, huh? Heart stopped sudden like?"

"That's it. Now, my boy" — Doc Grumman blinked his kindly eyes — "it's up to you to take charge. Jake Barry I've known for thirty years, and he hadn't any other relatives but you. So yuh're his sole heir and yuh ought to see to it that he's buried proper and all honors done. Just thought I'd tell yuh."

Hatfield started. "Good gosh!" he thought. "So I am, accordin' to Pecosville! I inherit all Barry's holdin's!"

That angle had failed to occur to him, because he was aware that he was only posing as Jake Barry's nephew, but the people of the vicinity believed him to be Barry's nephew.

"I'm not forgetting that attack on him the

first night I was here, either," he thought grimly.

Citizens, hearing of the mayor's death, were coming in to pay their last respects to Jake Barry.

"Anybody happen to see George Canty?" Hatfield asked.

"Yeah," a man replied. "He's been playin' poker with some of the boys all evenin' at the Prairie Fire Saloon. Ain't stirred out of there. I was in there myself since dinner time."

The citizen who spoke was a reputable man, owner of the general store and a friend of Barry's.

"Perfect alibi again," decided Hatfield. "As usual!"

Canty was taking no more such chances as he had before, when he had gone on trial for the murder of Jake Lee.

"He'll be after me hammer and tongs," thought Hatfield. "I've got to get to work pronto."

He again examined Barry. The cords stood out on the pallid face and neck, although rigor mortis had not yet fully set in.

Hurrying back, he told Bob Allison of Barry's death.

"Why," gasped Bob, "he must have — he —"

"Yeah," drawled Hatfield, "he must have been meetin' somebody who could tell him about George Canty, I reckon! Can't prove a thing on Canty, because he's been in sight all evenin', the way he was when Lee died. Now you lie low and be ready when I call yuh."

Picking up Goldy, Hatfield mounted and rode swiftly across the plaza to the Last Chance, a one-storied plank affair which was a Barry property. Only about twenty-five minutes had elapsed since Barry had been found there dead. The main saloon was empty save for the barkeep, for those customers who had been present had gone over to Barry's.

"Yeah, the mayor come in," the bartender told Hatfield, in answer to the Ranger's questioning, "and said he was meetin' a man in the last room, Number Four, on the left of the hall in back there. Didn't want to be disturbed, he told me. When I happened to be passin' the closed door, though, I heard a heavy thud, like a man fell, and a sort of funny gasp. I knocked and didn't get no answer, so I shoved in the door and there he was, lyin' dead in the middle of the floor."

The Ranger hurried through to the back, along a dim-lit, narrow corridor. Doors opened off from this, and the last on the left let him into a small, square room with a single little window, on which brown paper had been pasted to act as a shade. Some chairs, a table and a small oil lamp made up the furnishings.

As the Ranger paused in the door, his eyes sweeping the room, his alert gaze caught a slight movement at his right.

"By glory, that chunk of floor board shifted!" he thought.

A piece of the three-inch pine board flooring had moved slightly. He was not standing on a connecting plank, and —

Whirling, he tiptoed lightly to the back and quietly opened the door giving into Tin Can Alley. A faint clang sent him jumping to the left. He placed sounds in the blackness by the side corner, and his Colt leaped to his slim hand, ready for action.

"Look out — here he comes!" a man warned in a hoarse whisper.

Hatfield threw himself flat as a heavy gun roared a few feet from his eyes, the flashing powder half blinding him. He let go at the approximate position, heard a stifled curse, and heavy steps. There were men there, a number of them, and guns began bellowing his way, as he snuggled close to the foundation.

Bullets shrieked in the night, hunting him, as his ears were deafened by ringing explosions. Death was in his face, too many foes for him to take care of at the same time. They had better cover than he, and their lead, .45 slugs, and then scattering buckshot, cut up the dirt too close for comfort.

He squirmed back, making the open doorway where he was comparatively safe from the curtain of lead.

He waited, alert, listening as best he could, but the guns covered other sounds. Then their voices ceased, and he caught running steps in the side alley. Leaping to the turn, he was in time to glimpse a burly dark figure make the corner and swing right on the sidewalk.

Dashing through in pursuit, he saw plenty of men moving on the plaza and coming up the sidewalk toward the shooting. Mustangs tethered at the hitch-rail running along the curb were snorting and rearing, disturbed by the explosions.

But he could pick out no one suspicious. His enemies had made a quick second turn, no doubt along the adjoining alleyway, and were out of sight. He went back to the rear of the Last Chance and, kneeling at the side, struck a match, shading it in his hand.

Boarding ran lengthwise around the base

of the building, set on logs driven down through the sandy ground to bedrock, as were so many Western structures. The siding was loose and dried out. He easily pulled a board aside and, flattening out, found the soil cut up, disturbed, with deep indentations of knees and boots.

A sudden thought brought him upright.

"It ain't long till nine o'clock! Allison was to meet that party at the Buffalo Head then! They must be —"

He broke off, jaw setting. He was hot on the trail and getting hotter.

Avoiding citizens who were swarming through to find out what the rumpus was about, the Ranger whistled thrice. As he moved along Tin Can Alley, skirting piles of cans and refuse tossed from the back doors of saloons and stores, the golden sorrel, trained to come at his signal, galloped to him. He mounted and rode off.

He hit the dark chaparral past the town's south limits, and streaked around, out of sight of spying eyes in the settlement, until he could close in again on Barry's barn, where Bob Allison and his waddies waited.

"What's the word, Jim?" inquired Allison, eyes gleaming in the faint light that filtered from the house windows and the open kitchen door.

"Allison," said Hatfield, "I don't dare let yuh go to the Buffalo Head alone, as we planned. Our enemy's gettin' desperate, plannin' two killin's in one night. And they'll shoot it out in a pinch. They'd be able to riddle yuh in a lighted room. I nearly caught 'em outside the Last Chance just now, where Mr. Barry died, and that's what the firin' yuh heard was about. Yuh know where Room Six is at the Buffalo Head?"

"It's the last private room on the right as yuh go down the hall," replied the stalwart young foreman.

"*Bueno.* Get yore hosses and foller me. No noise, now."

Ready for action, the Square L outfit mounted behind Allison, and trailed the Ranger.

The Buffalo Head stood at the north end of Pecosville, on the same side of the plaza as Barry's home. Hatfield dismounted them outside the light circle and started in, guns ready.

"Down," whispered Hatfield, as they came within a couple of hundred yards of the rear of the saloon.

There were lights on in front, and Allison pointed out the small window, shaded by paper, which showed a low glow marking Room 6.

"They must be all set and waitin' for Allison by now," Hatfield muttered.

He knew that alert spies would be watching for any slip-up. There were sheds and stables between the back alley and the Buffalo Head, and Hatfield's position. He desired to get in closer, and whispered his orders to Allison to be ready at his call.

Spurs would clink and leather would rustle. A big Stetson loomed even against a dark background. So the Ranger slipped off boots, chaps and hat, and started crawling, flat on his belly, toward the saloon. He made a foot or two at a time, and reached the stable at last, sure he had not been observed.

Chapter XVIII:
Dog Fight

Peering around the right rear corner of the stable, Jim Hatfield could distinguish the shape of the window in Room 6 and the black smudge of the alley door. Some sounds came from the main saloon in front, and the voices of men from the plaza and streets.

But as he waited, he could see no one lurking about the back of the place.

Inching forward like a caterpillar, Hatfield kept a Colt in his right hand, ready for action. He drew in, nearer and nearer, ears seeking to filter any warning noises from the general welter of small clamor in Pecosville.

He lay flat, eyes hunting for sign in the darkened house which flanked the Buffalo Head on the same side as Room 6, but nothing stirred. Inching on, he came to the black shadow of the building, at the back. There were faint streaks in the alleyways and passages at the wings, leading out to the street.

He felt of the foundation, the same sort of flimsy board covering as he had encountered at the Last Chance. Working silently, he managed to pull a plank out far enough for him to squeeze under. He had about three feet leeway overhead, and as he crawled in sandy earth, spider webs and dry dirt soon covered his face and hands.

Figuring that he was under Room 6, in the complete blackness he had to depend entirely on his sense of touch. The stale odor of trapped air under the building did not help him.

"Oughta be right here," he thought, feeling about with his left hand.

After a few seconds, his fingers touched what he was hunting, the cool, rounded metal surface of a pipe.

The pipe was partially buried in the loose, sandy soil. Hatfield felt along its length until it passed under the wooden siding around the base of the saloon.

"They must have it hid altogether on the outside," he figured. "They could lay it mighty fast in this kind of dirt and a couple inches of buryin' would be enough for the time they'd need it. Could go anywheres they wanted with it in a few hours, too!"

Faintly there came to him a hollow, dim clang, running along the pipe. He decided that someone must have stepped on the pipe.

He tensed, staring at the blackness in front of him, but a few tiny cracks of light between the siding were all he could make out. Then he heard a faint creaking sound, to his left, and he flattened out.

"Get it out, pronto!" a hoarse whisper commanded. "The boss says so!"

Something had warned Canty. Perhaps it was because it was after nine, and Bob Allison had failed to show. Added to this, the encounter Hatfield had had at the Last Chance, the tigerlike instinctive caution of the well-digger, and that was enough to cause Canty to hide the evidence, give up his attempt on Allison for the time being.

Hatfield had no time to think of that now. They were almost upon him, and he saw the burly, black-shaped bulks of men looming in the opening they had made. They were crawling in under the house, to remove the pipe.

He let them get inside, counting four of them. But there were others outside, ready and waiting.

Suddenly a match flared in a cupped hand, because they needed light to work by, and the Ranger recognized the face of the man who held the little flame to the blackened wick of a dark-lantern.

It was Morg, the thin well-digger with the crooked nose that was twitching now. Morg worked for George Canty, as Hatfield knew.

"What the devil's that!" gasped the man hidden by Morg's scrunched-up body.

"What's what — quiet, yuh fool!" snarled Morg, looking around.

"Right ahead! It's a —"

"Throw yore hands out in front of yuh and lie still, boys," snapped Hatfield, "or yuh die!"

Morg uttered a startled yip and straightened up spasmodically, his head banging the crossbeam over him. It dazed him and he sprawled, close to Hatfield, who crouched there, gun up and the hammer back under his thumb. When he raised that thumb, the gun would fire!

His thumb flicked up. Morg and his mates did not obey his command, and the rustle of death was too close to ignore.

Morg took it in the top of the head, instantly killed as he sought to get a Colt from his belt. The blasting blare of the heavy revolver dominated the confined space under the saloon, as Hatfield whipped aside in a roll. Hasty slugs hunted him, but the

Ranger bullets cut flesh, drove the men out, helter-skelter.

"Square L, this way!" roared Hatfield.

Morg's body blocked the nearest exit. The Ranger had to crawl around it, and then he paused at the hole the retreating men had left.

He knew he had made other hits, but they were not fatal, and the dark foes he had encountered under the Buffalo Head split up and ran.

"Allison!" called the Ranger, hearing sounds to his left, in the direction of the stable.

"Yeah, here we are, Jim!"

Allison came dashing up, his waddies behind him, Colts out.

"Did yuh see 'em?" asked Hatfield.

"Yeah, one run up the alley! Who was it?"

"Well, there's a dead man underneath there — Morg, one of Canty's diggers. Come on! We'll reconnoiter Canty's place pronto. . . ."

Canty, hastily summoned from the Prairie Fire Saloon, where he was having a drink with Doc Grumman after leaving Barry's house, listened to the report of his frightened henchman, Lefty. The left arm of the short and stout Lefty was punctured, bleeding as he held it tight with his other hand.

Lefty was gasping for breath after his run. Besides he had heard Ranger lead close to his vitals and had felt the bite of it. He was an awesome figure as he made his swift report, clad in dark pants and shirt as he was, and with his cheeks smudged by burnt cork. The whites of his cow eyes rolled as he told his employer what had occurred.

"— and this Jim Barry devil was lyin' under there, waitin' for us, Boss!" he quavered, aware of the mounting fury in Canty's glinting gaze.

"Well — yuh mean six of yuh run from one man?" snarled Canty. "What'd yuh leave behind?"

"He's a plumb devil Boss! We left Morg there, dead, I reckon, 'cause he wasn't more'n four feet from Barry's gun. He never shifted after he dropped."

"The pipe — what about the pipe?" Canty snapped impatiently.

"We didn't get a chanct to pick it up. He was goin' to murder us all!"

Canty hit him, in the teeth, and Lefty cowered, sniffling.

"Grab a drink and hide yoreselves in the yard," snarled Canty. "Keep outa sight. This is bad."

He swung, lurching along with his crab-like gait. Up the alley, he reached his back fence, higher than a man's head. A locked gate was opened at his whispered hail and armed guards were waiting there. There were patrols making the circuit of the yard, and in the black shadows the piles of equipment made blacker ones.

"Where's Duke?" demanded Canty.

"He's takin' a nap," a man in a Stetson and cowboy garb replied.

Muttering curses, Canty went lumbering away.

CHAPTER XIX:
CANTY'S YARD

Georse Canty sidled to his kitchen door, where more armed men gathered, lounging about in the darkness.

He grunted at their greeting, and entered. Duke Varron roused as Canty shook his shoulder. The Lazy C chief was stretched on the bunk in a side room, snatching forty winks. He yawned, sitting up, blinking in the light of a shaded candle that burned on the table.

"What's wrong, Canty?" he complained.

"Plenty! Allison didn't show up at the Buffalo Head. I had a funny feelin' inside about that, and besides that Jim Barry devil was snoopin' too close to me. He nearly come up with the boys pickin' up the pipe at the Last Chance and when my men went to the Buffalo Head, there he was, waitin' under the saloon! He killed Morg, and wounded Lefty."

"The sidewinder!" faltered Varron, his

weak chin dropping. He bit at his crisp, neatly trimmed little mustache. "The — the jig's up, then! How the devil a feller like him could be so quick on the trigger beats me! He's Barry's nephew, ain't he, but what in thunder! A Texas Ranger couldn't do better!"

Canty gave a sharp exclamation.

"Duke! I wonder if yuh hit it! A Ranger! He might be. Lee sent for 'em, and to cover myself I did, too, after I heard he had. Anyways, Ranger or not, he's got to die and Allison along with him! They're all that stand in our way now. Check yore men, and get 'em ready. It's in the open, and we got to down that Jim son and Allison 'fore they spill the beans. They've snooped too close."

Canty was on edge, well aware of the menacing fate that was closing in on him. Craftily as he had managed affairs so far, he found the murder chain he had forged tightening with heavier coils about him.

He dared not draw back. To wait would be fatal, but he must lash out with full force, try to crush those who were so hot on his bloody trail.

"Allison, Jim Barry, and then any of them other ranchers who dare to buck me for a minute!" muttered Canty.

He would destroy them all rather than

relinquish his evil ambitions to dominate his fellowmen.

"Let's git goin', Duke," he snapped.

He seized the door latch and ripped open the door, burning with his hate of his opponents, stepping out into the yard, followed by Duke Varron.

He had no idea that even then the eyes of an avenger were on him, because he knew nothing of the men who had seen him enter this yard fortress. But in the black shadow across the dirt side street, Hatfield and Allison had reconnoitered, peering at Canty's high fence. A faint glow marked the position of the well-digger's home, while down the passageway, behind the two determined young men, were the Square L waddies, guns ready, waiting for their orders.

"That was Canty who just went in the rear gate," Allison had breathed at the moment the well-digger had entered the yard of his home.

"Yeah," whispered Hatfield. "He was no doubt warned by them hombres I tangled with at the Buffalo Head. It's likely to make him desperate, for he'll know how close we are to him. I've got to find out what he means to do, if I can. I'm goin' in and have a look-see. You stick here and be ready if I call."

Allison was astounded at the tall man's temerity, but he only said:

"All right, Jim. I'm with yuh."

Crouching low, using Indian stealth, Hatfield made the fence, pushing close to the base outside. Keen ears strained the sounds from within. Almost on him, from the other side of the fence, came a sentry's tread.

"I'll have to divert him," he decided.

As soon as the man went by, he ducked back and touched Allison.

"Go down opposite the fence corner, Bob, and toss a rock over so's to attract the guards inside. Stay out of sight, on this side of the street."

When Allison was set, Hatfield, again crouched at the base of the fence, waited until he heard a stone crash to his left. He heard the swift steps of a sentry go by on the other side of the fence and he straightened up, gripping the splintered top of the planks, and hoisting himself up.

He could now glimpse the gloomy interior of Canty's big enclosure, with the piles of pipe and other equipment cluttering it. To his left, the black figures of armed men were hustling to the corner where Allison's rock had hit.

He slid over the top and dropped into the yard. No outcry came, and a moment later, down low, he was behind a bulky pile of pipe, partially covered by a tarpaulin.

The sentries, finding nothing to do battle with, finally turned back to their posts. Hatfield, inching ever nearer to the back door, lay flat, snuggled to some lumber which was used by Canty for shoring the wells he dug. He could see the light in the back window, and the crack marking the door.

The door suddenly opened, and Hatfield, scrunching back and freezing to avoid being spotted in the channel of yellowish light that came from it, plainly saw George Canty. Duke Varron was right behind him.

He was so close that he could overhear Canty's harsh voice as the well-digger gave his orders.

"Sift yore men through the town, Duke, and shoot down Allison and that Jim Barry fool on sight! I'll have 'em tonight or know the reason why. Get goin', pronto."

Varron stepped forward, and softly called:

"Tiny — Arkansas — Lewis!"

He was summoning his gunny lieutenants to give them commands. The hard-faced, two-gunned men slid up, leather rustling.

"Get the boys ready for action," Varron ordered. "We're gunnin' for Bob Allison and that Jim Barry snake, on sight, savvy? The man who downs one of 'em or both gets a hundred extra dollars. If any Square L men or other ranchers try to stop yuh, let them have it, too. We ain't foolin'.."

The aides hustled to carry out Varron's commands.

"I'm goin' back and watch from the front, Duke," Canty growled. "Make shore there ain't no mistakes, now."

He went inside and shut the door. Hatfield sought to follow Varron with his eyes. Duke paused a few feet from him, and the faint rustle of crinkly paper told Hatfield that Varron was rolling a cigarette. A moment later, a match was struck and Duke stood within three yards of the Ranger's hiding-place, his weak-chinned face marked by the black blob of his tiny mustache was plain in the light.

Hatfield could not allow such an opportunity to pass. The gunnies were lining up at the back gate in formation, the guards still circled the inner fence, but there was no one close to Duke Varron.

The Ranger whizzed through the space between them as silently as an attacking panther. His powerful forearm circled Varron's throat, cutting off all cries save one muffled squeak of fright. His knees rammed into Duke's spine, paralyzing the man and knocking out his wind. In the terrific, vise-like embrace of the Ranger, Varron was as helpless as a baby.

Hatfield had him completely subdued when a blow from his free fist stunned the gunny chief.

With Varron slung over his shoulder like a sack of oats, Hatfield ran lightly toward the fence. He crouched beside the pipe until the sentry had passed, and his back was turned to Hatfield.

Canty's latch on the back door clanked again, and the well-digger appeared.

"Say, Duke," he called, "I forgot. Come back here a minute."

Hatfield had timed his seizure of Varron to the instant. He had just straightened up to ease Duke over the fence when Canty happened to appear. The guard swung at Canty's call and saw the dark shape of the Ranger, with Varron on his shoulder, standing by the fence, since the light shaft from the door marked him.

"Hey — who in thunderation is that!" sang out the guard, starting toward the Ranger, with his double-barreled shotgun rising.

Canty glanced over in the direction of the call, and other sentinels swung to the alert, facing Hatfield.

The Ranger had to think fast. Investigation would be fatal, and he wanted Duke Varron.

"Bob!" he roared. "Come get him!"

Allison would be listening, close at hand. By main force Hatfield heaved the limp Varron up, and threw him bodily over the top of the fence. He whirled, free of Duke's weight, and as the guard aimed the shotgun and fingered the first trigger, Hatfield threw himself flat, even as his own Colt flashed out.

The charge of buckshot, hunting him, spattered the fence against which he had been standing a breath before. Then, echoing the deep-throated *whoosh* of the scatter-gun, came the Ranger Colt. The sentinel screamed, folded back, kicking the ground.

The flashing powder exposed the Ranger's exact position. Canty leaped forward, down behind the pile of wood, calling orders.

"There he is!" yelled Canty. "Get him!"

Bullets began slapping into the fence boards, ripping through, kicking up the gravel and dirt underfoot. Hatfield was already moving, however. He could not climb the fence and frame his body against the lighter sky now, with the enemy weapons on him, so he dived behind the end of the pile of pipe, his Colts snarling back at his foes, holding them at bay.

"Can't stick here, though!" he muttered. "They'll run over me when they mass."

He seized a short length of the iron pipe and, holding it in his left hand and his Colt in his right, hunted with his eyes along the fence. He had downed the guard on that section, and only ten yards behind him, within a few feet of the board fence, stood a well-digging machine, offering some protection.

"Hey, Jim — are yuh all right?" Bob Allison was calling frantically to him above the din.

Canty recognized that voice. He was swearing a blue streak, realizing now against whom his men were fighting.

"It's Barry and that Square L foreman, boys!" he shouted furiously. "Make sieves of 'em!"

"Keep back, Allison!" bellowed the Ranger. "I'm doin' all right!"

He rushed, made the bulk of the machine. Without a breath of delay he seized the piece of pipe in both hands and rammed it hard against the foot-wide, upright fence board. Bullets searched for him, hitting the machine, the fence, and whistling in the air over him, but he drove the end of the pipe into the board, hands stinging at the impact.

The planks were embedded in the dirt,

but as the Ranger hit the one he had chosen, on the third try it cracked, splintered and sagged outward. He dropped the pipe then, seized his Colt. Blasts from his weapon answered his foes, as he turned sideward and pushed through the gap.

"He's got outside!" shrieked George Canty, beside himself with fury at the Ranger's escape. "Go after him! Where the devil is Duke?"

Hatfield dashed across the narrow street to the protection of the buildings there. Citizens, alarmed at the heavy shooting and yells, were opening their windows and doors, peeking out to see what went on.

"Hey, Jim, here we are!" called Bob Allison, looming in a passageway before the tall Ranger.

Hatfield was gasping for breath, and his hand was hot from the belching Colt.

"Yuh got Varron?" he demanded.

"Yeah. The boys are holdin' him in the back alley."

"Good. Let's get out of sight."

Bullets were blindly seeking them as they made the turn and ran down the passage.

"There they go!" a sharp-eyed gunny cried.

The back gate was already open and Canty's killers were streaking out, hot on the trail of Hatfield and his handful of men.

Line after line of gunmen appeared in the side street, and Canty's bull voice could be heard, egging them on.

"Make a circle, pronto — hosses!" Canty bawled.

CHAPTER XX:
BESIEGED

Fully determined to hold Duke Varron at all costs, Jim Hatfield meant to give not an inch. Duke Varron was coming to. He uttered a shriek, a shrill cry that marked their position.

"Yuh should have gagged him," growled the Ranger. "Tie a bandanna over his mouth now, Bob."

Bullets sang close, as the dark figures of their enemies swarmed in the street, while the swift *clop-clop* of hoofs told that they were being circled. Their own mounts were still two hundred yards off, up toward Main Street and the plaza.

"We'll have to find a hole to duck into," muttered Hatfield. "Mebbe we can hold 'em off till help gets organized."

His strategical eye picked a stable, which had a base made of thick native adobe bricks.

"In there, fellers!" he urged.

Dragging Varron by the collar, they made the square stable. Hatfield swiftly posted the few fighters he had at the two doors, at the side windows.

"Watch yoreselves, now, boys," he cautioned. "We can't afford to lose any men."

The infuriated killers had located them, and guns snarled at them. The base of the stable, however, broke the leaden pellets into a hail of metal that spattered harmlessly to the sides and into the air.

Hatfield, breath coming hard from his terrific exertions, held the door, his Colt picking away at those who dared draw close.

For minutes that dragged like hours the Canty gang tried for them, pressing in. Sudden flashes of fire warned the Ranger that Canty was tossing burning brands on the dry shingles of the roof. They would catch quickly, smoke them out.

Confusion of sounds was in their ears, the ringing explosions of shotguns, Colts and carbines, and the blood-curdling shrieks of the angry gunmen. Beyond, was the general noise of the town, and the cries of alarmed citizens.

Smoke began drifting down on them, and they could see a red glow spreading on the stable roof.

"We ain't got long in here," the Ranger

thought grimly, knowing that when they ran out, bullets would riddle them.

Dimly, then, he heard a strident voice, one that came between explosions:

"Allison! Square L! Where are yuh?"

"Square L, this way!" Allison's joyful tones roared. "Square L, this way!"

"Them ranchers have pulled in at last!" decided Hatfield jubilantly.

Allison crawled to him. "Jim, that's Ollie Norton callin'!"

Smoke was choking them, watering their eyes. The whole roof seemed afire.

"Call again to Norton," ordered Hatfield.

Allison's young voice was trained to rise over the thunder of the stampede and reach across the distances of the range. "Norton," he bellowed, "we're in the stable! This way, Square L!"

"There they go!" muttered Hatfield, coughing in the acrid smoke.

Burning splinters were dropping, and the heat was growing impossible to bear.

Riders, coming like mad from the street, drove into the passage, Colts roaring at the killers. Canty's men, making a stand for only a minute, began to draw back, splitting up, vaulting fences, and streaking off under the rancher guns.

Hatfield and his men, dragging the moaning Duke Varron with them, crawled from the burning stable. The red glow from the roof made a light over the whole scene, the blackened, twisted faces of the besieged showing the strain they had been under.

Ollie Norton, the Pruets, men from the VV, the Crooked T and the Box Y, thirty of them altogether, had pulled into town, heeding Allison's call in the letter sent at Hatfield's order.

Norton swung from his saddle.

"What's up, Bob?" he demanded.

"Canty and Varron have gone mad!" Allison gasped. "They killed Mayor Barry, and they killed Ed Lee, too, Norton! He didn't die a natural death!"

A waddy from Norton's outfit galloped in from the street.

"Say, Boss, they're holin' up in Canty's, most of 'em!" he reported.

"Throw a cordon round the yard and hold 'em there," Hatfield commanded.

Norton gave the orders. The Square L, the ranchers who had come to their aid, swiftly rode into a circle, and with their guns covered any escape that might be tried from Canty's. The guns died off, as the two parties separated.

Now the citizens of the town began pushing up, demanding to know what went on.

Wally Tate, the town marshal, a stout man with a brown walrus mustache, pressed forward, his silver badge glinting in the light. A crowd swiftly collected as the lead ceased to fly.

"What the devil's goin' on here — more of that range war?" growled Tate angrily. "Yore ranchers fightin' Canty agin'? Yuh can't do it, endangerin' the lives of citizens thisaway!"

"I'm a Texas Ranger, Marshal," Hatfield broke in, in his commanding voice. "I'll tell yuh all about it in a minute. S'pose you take the folks up to that open space where that vacant lot is and I'll be right with yuh."

Marshal Tate could see the silver star on the silver circle, pinned to the tall man's shirt. That emblem was known through Texas and it commanded the deepest respect.

"Yes, sir, Ranger!" he cried. Turning, he shouted, "Get movin', folks! The Ranger's in charge here. He'll talk to yuh in a jiffy."

Bob Allison had Duke Varron, whose eyes were round as moons and filled with abject fright, in charge. Hatfield swung with a scowl on Varron, ripping off the bandanna gag.

"Yuh won't want that now, Duke. Yuh're goin' to squeal and squeal loud. I know what Canty's game is, and yuh're too deep in it to miss the noose, unless I give yuh a good word for helpin' us."

Allison held Varron, but there was no need to fear Duke now. He was crushed. The terrible power of Jim Hatfield, the nearness of the hot fire, the shrieking lead had broken his nerve. Hatfield had counted on Duke's weak chin, and he was right.

"I — I'll do whatever yuh want, Ranger," whimpered Duke.

Hatfield spoke rapidly with Varron, checking up on all he had learned. He knew most of it, and Duke supplied connections, the answers to a few puzzling details.

Armed men were surrounding Canty's. The well-digger's lights were turned out and the place quiet, as the killers inside waited for attack.

With Varron in tow, Hatfield walked toward the lot where the people were gathered to hear him. A dusty, tired body of men came pushing along, at their head Sheriff Miles.

"Hey, Ranger!" he bawled. "We hit that Lazy C but there was only four men there! I got yore note!"

"Sorry I couldn't meet yuh, Sheriff, but I had to hustle back to town. If yuh'll dismount and listen to what I'm goin' to say, yuh'll savvy why."

"Just as yuh say, Ranger." Miles pushed back his Stetson, wiping the sweat from his tired brow.

He snapped a command, and his followers dropped reins and stiffly walked to join the gathering at the lot.

"Gents," began the Ranger when all were gathered, "I've got a story to tell yuh and it's quite a yarn."

He stood on a flat rock in the midst of a large gathering of citizens and ranchers, those not on guard around Canty's.

"I've got Duke Varron here, as a prisoner," he went on, "and he'll tell yuh that what I say is true, every word."

Varron crouched near him, fright twisting his weak face.

"Most of you know George Canty," continued Hatfield. "He's the man responsible for the so-called range war and the shootin's in the county. He's been diggin' wells all over the district, huntin' water, and a few months back he happened to strike a big well of natural gas.

"Natural gas is worth plenty, more'n gold, if there's enough of it to pay for pipin'. It's cheap fuel, for homes and for towns and for factories of all kinds. There's a couple of good-sized cities within a hundred miles of here, and pipin' it is easy. From what Varron tells me, there's gas wells all around, under the range to the north and under the town itself.

"The man who owns the land would own the gas, like other minerals. So the more he had, the richer he'd be. If he owned all the big range and the settlement, why he'd be able to sell out for millions of dollars. He'd be a king, and rollin' in money. Folks would look up to him, kowtow to him — and that's what Canty pined for. He's funny lookin', and queer, and the boys laughed at him some and fooled him about it, and he's mighty stuck on hisself. It made him boil inside, and he was determined to get even with the world and make it lick his boots.

"However, certain men stood in his way on this. He owns his land but there's no gas right under that. Most of Pecosville belonged to Mayor Jake Barry. The range is split up among several ranchers, but the Square L, Ed Lee's place, dominates the chief part. With Lee's Square L, Canty could have shut off the main water supply from the creek and forced the rest of the ranchers to sell out for a song.

"He was makin' his plans on how to handle it all when Lee sent his son Jack and Allison to dig a water well for their steers in a distant section of their range. They happened to start right over a spot where Canty had probed, and where he knew there was a big collection of natural gas. If they hit it, he would lose his chance of bein' king.

"That's why he gunned young Lee and Allison. He forced Duke Varron in on it, knowin' of Duke's outlaw past. Duke was to split with him, so Duke furnished Canty with that fake alibi that saved him at the trial.

"Then Varron's men and Canty's begun tryin' to drygulch anyone else standin' in their way. The range war made a good excuse for such dirty work."

Men were listening tensely, some of them growling in their throats. "Varron tells me that Canty figgered on marryin' Lee's daughter, and gainin' the Square L through her," Hatfield went on, bursting another bombshell. "I told yuh he's stuck on hisself, and he was shore she'd have him, with Allison and her dad out of the way. He had some deeds and notes forged, with Mayor Barry's signature, so's he could seize on Barry's important properties after the mayor was killed.

"But, seein' he was under suspicion, and had to keep his nose clean so's he could enjoy the riches he wanted, he had to start workin' quiet-like, to throw off the law and folks watchin' him. He had a capped gas well under a shed he rented from Barry in town, and he run pipes, durin' the dark, to certain rooms where he lured Big Ed Lee, and Mayor Barry, and tried to get me and Allison. He picked spots he could easy reach and rooms where he could stop up what cracks there was. That's how he killed Barry and Lee, with natural gas, which has no odor, unless chemists put in some to warn folks.

"I was shore puzzled when Canty tried for me the first night I spent here, at Barry's, seein' as how I'd said I was Barry's long-lost nephew and had worked it easy enough. Then when I found what Canty was plannin', I figgered he'd got excited when an heir to Barry showed up. Duke told me just now that Canty was goin' to capture me and my hoss, have us disappear, and then blame Barry's death on me, his rascally nephew who robbed him."

Hatfield paused. Speeches were not in his line, but he had to make clear to them the monstrous Canty's crimes — and believed he had done it.

A growl began in the gathering, as men realized how horrible the well-digger was. It mounted in volume, and became a furious roar, the roar of a lynch mob.

"Rope!" bellowed a big cowman. "Get ropes and we'll hang Canty and the whole passel of 'em in the plaza!"

Lariats were quickly produced. Hatfield, spiriting Duke Varron out of the way and leaving him in Allison's charge, hurried over to Canty's front gate.

"Canty," he called, "yore goose is cooked! They're comin' after yuh to lynch yuh all! Yuh got one chance. Surrender to the Rangers and I'll protect yuh."

A bullet whirled over the crouched officer's head.

"Go in and get 'em!" the mob leader shrieked, from the plaza. The mob was surging forward.

Varron's men were in there also, listening, their nerve cracking. Hatfield, sheltered by a stone hitch-post outside Canty's, called to them over the fence,

"If you men shoot it out, yuh'll be hung! If yuh throw in yore guns and surrender, yuh got a chance of gettin' off with prison."

The mob was starting for the gates. Suddenly the front one opened, and one of Duke Varron's men leaped out, hands high.

"I quit, Ranger!" he cried.

One after another, the gunnies came forth. Varron was gone and his gunmen hated the noise of the mob.

"Line up along the fence and keep quiet," ordered Hatfield.

He swung, facing the oncoming citizens. Tell, erect, cool, the Ranger's eyes were as dark as an Arctic sea as he watched the mob.

"Keep back!" he called his voice ringing but quiet. "These are Ranger prisoners boys."

The mob paused, none of the men in it wishing to buck the Ranger. He waited a few moments, as silence came over them and the mob spirit began to wane.

"Look out!" someone shrieked.

Crashing through the open gate, ducking low over a powerful black, George Canty spurred, gun in hand. He fired into the crowd, using the assembled people as a screen, his only hope of escape.

Hatfield whirled, his slim hand flashing to his Colt with the speed of legerdemain. Canty was almost upon him, his evil face distorted with his insane fury, his cat-eyes glowing with feral intensity.

"Curse yuh, Ranger!" he shouted, his pistol hunting the man who had crushed him.

Hatfield's gun snapped first, thumb rising from the cocked hammer. Canty's horse slewed, and the red-haired well-digger was thrown violently off. But he came up, snarling, seeking to kill. Hatfield's second shot drove into the center of the man's breast, and the charging Canty threw up his arms and crashed forward on his face, stretched until he touched the Ranger's boots.

Jim Hatfield finished his report, as Cap'n McDowell listened in fascination to the end. "By jigs, that Canty was a tough one, Jim," he growled.

Back in Austin, at Ranger Headquarters Hatfield had told the strange story of Pecosville in full to his superior.

"Allison and that pretty Lee girl are gettin' hitched sir," Hatfield said. "They're safe now, and mighty well off, with all that natural gas under their range. They expect to keep the Square L and run it together. Barry's holdin's go the county and will be used for the public good."

Captain McDowell rose. "Yuh done a mighty fine job, Jim," he growled. "I'm proud of yuh. If I'd had any idea what yuh was runnin' into out there, I'd have sent more men with yuh. I can't afford to lose yuh. Like this job from the Border that just come in. It'll take an army, I reckon."

Hatfield's eyes grew interested. "What is it, sir?"

He heard, and soon he was on his way again, headed for the border on the golden sorrel, carrying the law of the Rangers to the far reaches of the Lone Star State.

We hope you have enjoyed this Large Print book. Other Thorndike, Wheeler, Kennebec, and Chivers Press Large Print books are available at your library or directly from the publishers.

For information about current and upcoming titles, please call or write, without obligation, to:

Publisher
Thorndike Press
10 Water St., Suite 310
Waterville, ME 04901
Tel. (800) 223-1244

or visit our Web site at:

http://gale.cengage.com/thorndike

OR

Chivers Large Print
published by AudioGO Ltd
St James House, The Square
Lower Bristol Road
Bath BA2 3SB
England
Tel. +44(0) 800 136919
email: info@audiogo.co.uk
www.audiogo.co.uk

All our Large Print titles are designed for easy reading, and all our books are made to last.

DATE DUE

FEB 03 '2012		
4-23-14		
3-5-16		
3.26.16		
4-23-16		
4.15.19		
5.15.19		